Coop's Corner
COLLECTION

Inspirational Stories and Poems

William M. Cooper

Strategic Book Publishing and Rights Co.

Strategic Book Publishing and Rights Co.
12620 FM 1960, Suite A4-507
Houston TX 77065
www.spbra.com

ISBN: 978-1-63135-757-2

Hardcover version published in 2015.
Softcover version published in 2012

𝔇𝔢𝔡𝔦𝔠𝔞𝔱𝔢𝔡 𝔗𝔬

Weldon and Evelyn are my parents. They died before they could leave a legacy that others could recognize. I should like to mention their long hours of personal sacrifice in providing for their children; to ensure we had shelter, cloths, food, along with proper academic, moral and religious instruction. Thank you Mom and Dad for all you did for me that I failed to recognize while you were still alive and forgive me for not honoring you until after it was too late.

And likewise, I'd like to honor and thank those readers of this book. I dedicate this book to your pursuits and legacies that depend on goodness. This book is to everyone who still believes in morality and who personally pursues righteousness because they know it is the best path to follow. To those who understand the differences between what's good and evil, right and wrong and who dedicates themselves and their children to noble character. To the wise of heart who thoroughly reviews books before recommending them or giving them as gifts.

To all my coworkers at Upstaging Inc. I hope this book blesses your socks off. Be Inspired!

Contents

Contents

Preface

Welcome friends and thank you for coming by Coop's Corner. I'm confident that my little corner store has something inspirational just for you. So by all means, do as all my other visitors have done and take your time shopping for that perfect story that speaks personally to you. Also, I've expanded my store and you can find a story poem section in the back. There's no telling what's inside waiting for you to discover. One more thing: could you do the old man a grand favor by telling all your friends about this place? We run the same special, which for one low price, you get every product stocked inside Coop's Corner. Your help has already made this store of ideas a great success.

I'm glad you came by for a visit and you can always drop in anytime you'd like.

Take care, everybody.

Yours truly,
Coop

Short Stories

The Mule and the Tractor

Chapter One: Home Sweet Home

"*Cock-a-doodle-doo*," cried Sonic Boom, the rooster. "Okay, everybody, it's time to get up. Time for roll call, you sleepy heads," Sonic Boom continued.

One-by-one, the animals sounded back their presence when their names were called.

As Sonic Boom went through the list, he discovered that someone was missing. Going through the roll call list once more, Sonic Boom repeated himself by saying, "Now let me see here; we have Fetch the dog, Sparkle the goldfish, Quacker the duck, Moocher the cow, Spit Fire the Mule, and his nephew, Rufus. I said, his nephew, Rufus!" Sonic Boom continued to call for Rufus over and over again until Rufus finally cooperated with him.

"Howdy everybody," said Rufus as he stuck his head out of the barn.

"About time you replied," said all the animals.

With roll call being over, the animals got in position for their favorite activity of the day, which was breakfast.

Rufus headed over to the bucket that the farmer kept tied to the fence post. The farmer always met him there every morning with a large can of honey-coated oats. As the farmer reached over the fence to pour the oats into the bucket, he scratched Rufus on his forehead and behind his ears. Rufus was in mule heaven with his favorite breakfast and a massage. Oh, how wonderfully sweet the honey was that coated his oats.

"Well, old boy, it was fun working with you," said the farmer in a sad tone to Rufus.

I wonder what he meant by that? Rufus thought to himself as he continued munching on his crunchy oats. Raising his head out of the bucket, Rufus said to the other animals, "I hope the farmer isn't going on another vacation with his wife."

Moocher lifted her head from her oats and said, "Why do you

say that, Rufus?"

"Because," said Rufus as he struggled to eat and talk at the same time, "the last time they left for a few days, somebody else came to feed us and they wouldn't show up until mid-day."

After tying a hat on Rufus's head, the farmer busied himself feeding the rest of us only after he was sure we had plenty to eat would he return to his house and have breakfast with his wife.

Chapter Two: Retired at the Age of Three

After our wonderful breakfast, Rufus went to the barn to find himself a fresh strand of straw that he could use as a toothpick. While he was in there, a loud engine noise filled the air with its heavy mechanical sounds. Rufus poked his head out of the barn for a glance and there in the driveway was a truck that had another machine riding on its back. All the animals lined up against the pen and watched with curiosity how the machine was unloaded. Since the tractor was parked on the lawn, Rufus decided he would take a closer look at it. Lifting the latch on the gate, Rufus strolled over to the tractor and began sniffing it. After a few quick sniffs, Rufus began crying out in mule language to us about how yucky he thought it was.

"What does it smell like?" asked Moocher.

Rufus replied, "It smelled like rubber, gas, oil, paint, and plastic."

"Sorry, old boy," exclaimed the farmer, "but this is what I was trying to tell you this morning when I told you how fun it had been working with you." Rufus' mouth hit the ground as the farmer continued explaining. "You see, Rufus, this tractor is how I'm going to plow the fields from now on. You have done your part for the farm, but now it is time for you to retire to the pasture with your uncle, Spit Fire."

As the farmer hopped on the tractor and drove away, Rufus began to cry in mule language. The rest of us farm animals were shocked at the news and did what was right by joining Rufus in his moment of grief. The farmer thought we were making the noises because we were afraid of the tractor, but we were crying for our friend, Rufus, who just lost his job.

Sonic Boom called out, "Attention all animals, we have an emergency meeting at the water trough in two minutes. I repeat: there will be a water trough meeting in two minutes."

The animals made their way to where I lived at the water trough. Each animal was determined to contribute his ideas in hopes that a solution could be made to help Rufus. Not only was I the speaker of the trough, but I was also the farm historian and psychologist.

Sonic Boom continued his announcements by saying, "Ladies and gentlemen of the assembly, please rise for Sparkle, Lady Speaker of the Trough."

I nodded to them all and then instructed them to be seated. I opened the meeting by saying, "Ladies and gentlemen of the assembly, today we meet to discuss what actions should be taken in order to repel the invasion of the tractor to our fair community. Having found the tractor guilty of impersonating a plow mule and thus having Rufus wrongfully retired, I move that suggestions be made by the assembly on what to do with this tractor."

Fetch jumped up and barked out, "I will go and bite the tires and flatten them so the tractor will have a hard time moving in a straight line."

Then Moocher mooed out, "I will go and ram the tractor with my horns and break it into a million pieces."

Quacker joined in and said, "My beak is sharp and I can chew the wires in half so it will stop running."

Rufus said in upset donkey language, "A good kick by these hind hoofs of mine should break it."

As the ideas continued to be expressed by all the animals, Spit Fire's voice came from behind them saying, "Those ideas sound good, but they will not work against the tractor."

"Uncle Spit Fire," yelled everybody with excitement. "Boy, are we glad to see you here," we all said happily.

Spit Fire trotted a little bit closer to us and then began to tell us just how indestructible the tractor was. Spit Fire said, "You will discover, Fetch, that the tires are thicker than your fangs, and the shell of it, Moocher, is much harder than your horns. The wires that dangle from the side, Quacker, have a special kind of insulation on them that nothing can chew through, and you, Rufus, will only knock your shoes off and possibly injure your hoofs before you get close to putting a small dent in it."

"What can we do?" we asked with concerned looks on our faces.

Spit Fire stood as erect as he could as he replied back, "There is only one thing you can do against the tractor, my friends, and that is to prove to the farmer that you can plow more than the tractor can. Once the farmer realizes that Rufus is better at plowing than the tractor, he will retire the tractor and put Rufus back into the work force."

The animals gave a standing ovation for Spit Fire's excellent suggestion and then they turned and began to chant, "Rufus! Rufus! Rufus!" Rufus turned his hat down toward his nose and with a stern look on his face, marched off to the barn to prepare for the plow-off contest.

Chapter Four: Let the Race Begin

Moocher sounded the alarm as she gave a low *moo* that resembled the sound of a ship horn wailing in the distance. Uncle Spit Fire accompanied Rufus and helped him put on his plowing gear. Piece after piece, the equipment went onto Rufus's body, very similar to King Arthur having his armor strapped on him by his armor bearer. Sonic Boom grabbed his beak and played a trumpeting tune generally played for royalty. Rufus snapped his hind hooves together and offered his salute to the assembled crowd of spectators. Placing the plow on his right shoulder, he turned on his heel and headed off to the field where the tractor was.

At the field, Rufus sank the plow deep into the ground and then row after row he pulled it, hoping that the farmer would reinstate him to his old job. The tractor was kicking up so much dust, however, that Rufus began choking.

"I should plow closer and ahead of the dust cloud," Rufus said to himself.

At the edge of the field grew a large mulberry bush and it was there that Rufus hid himself so he could surprise the farmer and get his attention. Rufus sprang out from behind the bush, which startled the farmer. In an effort to miss hitting Rufus, the farmer swerved the tractor. The farmer thought he had fallen asleep at the wheel and only dreamed Rufus had jumped out in front of him. Unknown to the farmer, Rufus was behind him, running the race of his life. Rufus caught up with the tractor and before the farmer could react to get away from Rufus, the two plows they were both pulling clipped each other, which caused the tractor to jolt. The farmer was ejected out of his seat, where he landed safely onto the freshly plowed soil. At the very instant that the farmer was ejected, Rufus was slung up into the air and landed in the driver's seat of the tractor. With both front hooves firmly gripping the steering wheel, Rufus began to laugh hysterically, because the tractor was going wherever he steered it to go. It was only after Rufus experienced plowing the field with the machine that he was finally able to understand just how useful the tractor was to the farmer. Rufus no longer resisted the idea of being retired because he was honest enough to accept the fact that the tractor could do a lot more work in a much faster time than he ever could.

Rufus thought to himself, *There is no good reason why I should fear the farmer wanting to change some things around here. He has worked hard for many years and now he has found an easier and smarter way to do the job. Besides, driving a tractor is far better than dragging a heavy plow.*

Chapter Five: Peace in the Valley

"*Cock-a-doodle-do*," cried Sonic Boom the next morning. Sonic Boom continued by stating, "Okay, guys and gals, it is time for our new exercise routine. Everybody bend and touch your toes. Now, give me some serious jumping jacks. And lastly, let's do some push-ups. Great job everybody," Sonic Boom said as he dismissed them.

No one ever complained about doing morning exercises because we all knew that this was Sonic Boom's way of showing us he cares about our health.

It was important to the farmer and his wife that we ate a good breakfast so they gave us fresh hay, oats, pellets, dog food, and a few dashes of fish food for me. Life was good on the farm and life got better now that the farmer and Rufus didn't have to work so long and hard plowing the fields.

"Well, Rufus, what are you going to do with all the extra time you have on your hands?" asked Fetch.

"I think I will become a famous artist and paint what I see and feel," explained Rufus.

"Oh," said Quackers, "we have an artist in our midst."

"Yes," said Rufus, "and with the extra time I have, I will use it to be creative and express myself."

The Mule and the Paint Brush

Chapter One: Home Sweet Home

"*Cock-a-doodle-doo*," cried Sonic Boom, the rooster. "Okay, everybody, it's time to get up," said Sonic Boom impatiently. "Time for roll call," Sonic Boom continued.

One-by-one, the animals sounded their presence when their names were called. As Sonic Boom went through the list, he read each name out loud and waited for a voice to call back stating, "I'm here!"

"Now let's see here," said Sonic Boom. "We have Fetch the dog, Sparkle the goldfish, Quackers the duck, Moocher the cow, Spit Fire the mule, and his nephew, Rufus." With roll call being over, the animals began their day with stretching exercises followed by an energy packed breakfast that the farmer provided right on schedule.

Because Rufus was retired, he had too much time on his hands. Rufus literally had nothing to do but eat oats and talk to his friends as they came by. Now that the farmer had a fancy new tractor to do all the plowing, Rufus felt useless and wanted so badly to somehow leave a legacy behind that would say to all who saw it, "Rufus was here." Rufus knew that he would some day be fully retired to the field with his uncle, Spit Fire. Rufus decided that he would follow his dream of being a world famous painter, so he stood up on his hind legs and stated quite regally, "Ladies and gentlemen, friends of the farm, be it known to all today that your very own Rufus will be changing his career from plow mule to painter of masterpieces."

There was no applause, no laughs of joy, just a bewildered look on each farm animal's face. *Oh, no,* they thought to themselves, *what is Rufus getting into now?*

Chapter Two: The World's Largest Canvas

After breakfast, Rufus went to the barn to find a paint brush and some paint and was lucky enough to find more paint than he needed for his project. There was blue, green, orange, yellow, red, black, and white paint — all in cans just waiting for Rufus to get busy with his new hobby.

Rufus pondered about what would be a good subject to paint. Minutes felt like hours as Rufus struggled over what would be worthy enough to be shown to the entire world in paint. All of a sudden, Rufus got the perfect idea. "My legacy will be about those I care about. I will paint portraits of my friends," he concluded. "Now then, what can I use for canvas?" Rufus pondered. "The barn, the barn!" Rufus shouted with joy. "The barn, the barn, the barn," he continued chanting.

Stroke after stroke, Rufus painted and he got so wrapped up in his work that he forgot to eat lunch and dinner. All through the day, Rufus worked until daylight had vanished and all his friends were asleep.

Rufus thought, *It is too late to show my masterpiece tonight, so tomorrow will be a big surprise for all of my friends.* Rufus went to bed exhausted, but also very excited and happy about his big wake-up surprise for all of his friends. "This was the best night I can ever remember," Rufus said to himself. He continued thinking happy thoughts like: *Boy howdy, will everybody be shocked when they see their faces on the side of the barn tomorrow?*

Rufus finally went to sleep, but in his dreams, he dreamed of stepping out of a long white limousine and onto a plush red carpet. On both sides of the carpet would be photojournalists with cameras flashing and reporters hoping for a chance to interview him. Rufus continued to dream of the awards ceremony where he would be recognized on global TV. There would be an auction that would follow the ceremony, where Rufus dreamed his paintings would sell for millions of dollars.

Chapter Three: The Secret Water Trough Meeting

That night, while Rufus was dreaming about the success of his painting, the farm animals assembled by the water trough. Sonic Boom had already flown to all the animals and announced that a secret water trough meeting was to be held after Rufus went to sleep. The animals were addressed by Sparkle the goldfish who lived in the water trough.

"Friends," said Sparkle, "we are gathered here tonight to discuss Rufus and the paintings he has made of us. As you all know," Sparkle continued, "Rufus does not know how to paint, but come tomorrow, if we show any disliking to his work, it will surely cause us to hurt his feelings. Are there any suggestions from the assembly concerning our actions tomorrow?"

Fetch was the first to come forward and he began by saying, "I'm not sure how you suppose that I pretend to like how Rufus painted me when he has me looking more like a badger than a dog."

Just as soon as Fetch finished talking, Moocher came forward and in a low voice said, "I agree with Fetch. How can we act like we are impressed with Rufus' paintings of us when they are so bad and we look so terrible in them?"

One-by-one, the animals' heads nodded in agreement as each animal came forward and made their complaint of not liking how they were painted.

After all the animals offered their complaints about how they did not like their painted pictures, the time came for the closing comments to the meeting.

Sparkle positioned herself in a way that the moonlight would show her clearly to them all. Sparkle said kindly and softly, "Dearest friends, I invited you here tonight, not to hear your complaints about how badly Rufus painted you, but to make sure that you didn't do to Rufus tomorrow what you have just done to me. You all saw how hard Rufus worked on this painting project and how long he painted in order that each of you had a portrait before he went to bed. While you were eating lunch and dinner and playing, Rufus, with joy in his heart, kept on painting into the night. While you were doing your daily activities, Rufus was busy for your sakes, making something special and nice that he could give to you. Even while

Rufus thought you were asleep, he refused to go to sleep himself, so he could honor you with a painting from his very own hooves. Rufus didn't just paint today; in truth, he loved each of us in his own special way with something he felt would make us happy. Now, I ask you one-and-all: do we dare take such a loving act as Rufus has done and call it ugly or bad? I call you to your senses and ask you all to look at these paintings tomorrow with your hearts and not just with your eyes."

One-by-one, the animals hung their heads in shame for being so blind to the goodness of their old friend, Rufus. As the water trough meeting closed, all of the animals' hearts were changed and they were convinced that Rufus deserved better from them.

Chapter Four: Gale Force Rescue

Roll call came quickly the next morning. The farm animals couldn't wait to see Rufus and ask him for a chance to view their pictures. Each one had trouble sleeping that night because they couldn't wait to see Rufus and tell him something good about the paintings and for all his hard work that he had put forward on their behalf.

As Rufus stood before them with a giant smile on his face, he decided that the only fair way to allow them to see their picture was to draw straws. Just as soon as the straws were all drawn, a strong wind blew across the field and into the barn area. The wind was so strong that all the animals held onto a portion of the fence to keep from being blown away. There was a loud, destructive noise and to everyone's amazement the barn was flattened to the ground.

Rufus and the other animals exploded in loud noises of unhappiness. The farmer and his wife ran outside to see what the problem was, and to their shock, they saw that the barn was destroyed.

Sonic Boom sounded out an emergency roll call and found that all the barn animals were present and safe. Each animal consoled Rufus with hugs and comforting words about the loss of his portrait gallery. They all admitted that they really wanted to see the paintings that he had made for them. Sadly, all the animals thought about how unfortunate it was that they would never get the chance to see the pictures Rufus made for them and tell him what a great job he did.

The farmer came over with the tractor and began taking the barn apart. The farmer's wife led the animals to a safer place where they could play away from the damaged barn. Each board from the barn had the nails pulled from it and then was neatly stacked into a pile.

The next day, the farmer had a crew show up and they built a brand new metal building where the old barn used to stand. While the crew was erecting the metal barn, the farmer took the scrap lumber from the old wooden barn and started patching up the pig pen with it. The pen was only a stone's throw away, so the animals stood and watched the farmer. Along with fixing the fence that made the pen, the farmer also built a bigger shelter to help keep the sun off the pigs.

"Look," cried Quackers the duck.

"Wow," said the rest of the animals.

Sparkle began jumping out of the water trough, shouting, "I can't see a thing!"

Rufus ran over to the water pump and began filling up the trough. When the water reached the edge, Sparkle stuck her head out of the trough and said, "Oh, I see it and it is truly beautiful, Rufus."

Oinkers the pig squealed out a thank you to Rufus for the much needed improvements to his pen. Oinkers said, "I would have been happy with some old planks, but the Picasso was a nice, extra touch."

The farmer, by sheer accident, had used all of the painted boards from the barn and mixed them up in the repair job. What was a very questionable portrait yesterday became the pride and joy of the farm for years to come.

"What a neat painting," said Fetch.

"What a great job you did," said Moocher.

Sonic Boom crowed out a "You can paint me anytime, Rufus."

There was a steady drip coming from the water trough as Sparkle was crying tears of joy because she was so happy that everything turned out so well.

Rufus was glad that he did not lose his paintings completely and he was also glad that his friends got to see them. Oinkers the pig was also glad because he not only got to see the paintings for himself, but he also got a better home out of the disaster. Life was good once again on the farm.

Rufus decided to go and get more paint so he could paint the new barn, but discovered that he had used it all up. As Rufus was walking away sulking over not having any more paint, he accidentally bumped into a rake that was leaning up against the wall. *Clang, clang, clang, clang*, sounded the rake as it scraped by each metal rib on the wall on its way to the ground.

"What was that noise?" asked Uncle Spit Fire. "Is the confounded barn falling down again?"

"No, Uncle," said Rufus, "it was a rake that I knocked over." Rufus grabbed the rake again and leaned it up against the wall and let it slide down to the ground. *Clang, clang, clang, clang,* went the rake again as it banged against the barn wall. "Cool," said Rufus. "I'm inspired by the sound of the rake and the beat it makes as it falls to the ground."

Spit Fire and the other animals gasped quietly as they thought, *Here we go again!*

The Mule and the Rake

Chapter One: Home Sweet Home

"*Cock-a-doodle-doo,*" cried Sonic Boom, the rooster. "Okay, everybody, it's time to get up," said Sonic Boom to all the barn animals. "Time for roll call once again," Sonic Boom continued.

One-by-one, the animals stood in line facing what seemed to be a military drill instructor in a rooster's costume, each one sounding back when their names were called.

Sonic Boom went through the list of names as though it were a mile long. "Let's see here," said Sonic Boom, "we have Fetch the dog, Sparkle the goldfish, Quackers the duck, Moocher the cow, Rufus the mule, and his uncle Spit Fire."

With roll call finally over, the animals followed Sonic Boom as he called out exercises for them to do. After their early morning workout, the animals enjoyed a wonderful breakfast that the farmer provided them. The animals came to really appreciate the goodness of the farmer and his wife and how they were always there for them every day. Good weather or bad weather never kept the farmer from showing up at the same time every morning and every afternoon in order to feed the animals wholesome meals and fresh hay to snuggle up in when it was bed time or cold outside.

The animals were also good to the farmer and everything that they did was intended to show him their appreciation. Sonic Boom faithfully called to wake the farmer every morning when the sun was coming up and he gave the alarm when any predators were near. Sparkle kept the water trough clean so all the animals had fresh water. Quakers gave eggs so the farmer and his wife could also have breakfast and make cakes. Fetch gave the farmer company when he was outside. Several times already, Fetch saved the farmer from a snake that was about to bite him. The farmer was able to make many good things to eat from Moocher's daily milk. Why even old Spit Fire kept the grass and weeds down in the other pen so the farmer wouldn't have to mow it so often. Actually, the only person who didn't have something to do was Rufus. He was almost bored to tears because he had gone from a plow mule to a painter and was now a do-nothing.

Doing nothing is harder than doing something, Rufus thought. Because there wasn't much going on in the pen, Rufus decided to take a stroll to see if he could find a project that would occupy his mind.

Rufus was walking around the barn when he accidentally knocked over a rake that was leaning up against the wall. *Clang, clang, clang*, sounded the rake as it fell hitting the metal bends in the wall.

"Oh, what is this?" asked Rufus to himself. "I have never heard such wonderful sounds in all my mule days."

Rufus picked the rake up and let it drop down again. He liked it so much that he kept picking it up and letting it bang its way down to the ground. Annoyed by the high pitch of the clanging noises, Fetch went over to Rufus to investigate what was going on.

"Hi, Rufus," Fetch said.

"Oh, hi Fetch," Rufus replied back with a smile and then dropped the rake again. The clanging sounds hurt Fetch's ears so much that he sat back and began to howl. Rufus, not knowing that dogs howl when their ears are hurt by noises, mistook Fetch's howling for singing and dropped the rake even more.

When Sonic Boom heard the clanging noises and Fetch howling, he mistook it all for a predator and began crowing as loud as he could to send out an alarm. This caused Quackers to go into a flapping frenzy, which encouraged Rufus to make even more clanging noises. All of this upset Moocher so badly that she began mooing and banging around in her stall. With total chaos in the barn, Sparkle was unable to determine what the problem was and, because everybody was screaming, she feared the worse and began to cry.

Rufus was in mule heaven as he saw everyone enjoying his musical talent. His mind drifted off into a daydream where he dreamed he was in a famous band. He could see himself sitting behind a huge set of drums playing hard and fast for thousands of fans shouting as he played. He was flattered to see so many cute she mules on the front row cheering for him. As Rufus was soaking in the wonder of his dream, he was suddenly snapped out of it by a splash of cold water that the farmer tossed on his head.

The animals scattered in a flurry leaving Rufus and the farmer alone.

"It seems you need something to do, Rufus," said the farmer

with a smile on his face. The farmer continued talking to Rufus saying, "Ever since I retired you from plowing, you have been getting into all kinds of trouble and now you have the whole farm in an uproar. Starting tomorrow, I'm going to find you something useful to do."

Rufus wasn't sure what the farmer meant, but he knew the farmer well enough to know that he was in for a real workout come the next day.

Chapter Three: Never an Idle Moment

The farmer was up earlier than usual and was already setting out the feed before any of the animals were up. By the time Sonic Boom crowed to wake every body up, the farmer had already put Rufus in the trailer in order to get to town on time.

At the county fair, the farmer and his wife set up a children's ride. Rufus had a saddle on his back and child after child lined up for their ride. Rufus couldn't believe what he was being asked to do and began to cry out in donkey language.

The farmer was unable to get Rufus to move, but his wife got out a carrot and gave it to Rufus and whispered in Rufus's ear saying, "I've got more where that one came from. Be a good boy and you'll get the whole bag." Rufus hopped into action and began to walk out each ride as though he was getting a carrot for every step he took. As Rufus looked at all the faces of the children, he began to figure out what was going on. He looked back over his shoulder at the little girl that was on his back and how she had the biggest smile he had ever seen on a person. "Wow!" said Rufus to himself. "These little farmers think I'm great to be on." This made Rufus forget about his carrots because now he was working for the happiness of the children.

After half the day was over, the farmer and his wife loaded up everything and rode back to the farm. Rufus was tired, but he was glad that he got to make so many people happy, considering just yesterday he made so many others sad with all of his clanging noises.

Rufus thought he was through for the day, but the farmer led him out to the field dragging a long chain. The farmer wrapped the chain around a stump and then attached the other end of the chain to the rigging that was strapped around Rufus.

"Pull, boy, pull," said the farmer as he patted Rufus on his hindquarters.

Rufus cried out in mule language, "This is hard, this is hard, this is hard, this is hard."

The farmer didn't try to make Rufus be quiet because he knew the stump was going to be difficult to pull out of the ground.

All the animals were at the edge of the barnyard fence watching and calling out to Rufus not to give up.

Oinkers crawled out of his mud pit to shout for Rufus and said, "Make us proud, Rufus."

Fetch barked out, "Don't give up, Rufus."

Moocher mooed, "Put your back into it."

Sonic Boom crowed, "Show them who is boss."

Quackers quacked, "Show us how it's done."

I said softly and affectionately, "We believe in you, Rufus."

With that final word of encouragement, Rufus pulled the stump out of the ground and dragged it to the burn heap.

By then it was dark and the farmer took Rufus back to the barn. As the farmer wiped Rufus down with a towel, he said to him, "Rufus, old boy, you did good today. I'll be back tomorrow morning to fetch you again, so be sure to get your rest."

Rufus was scared that the farmer was going to work him that hard every day for the rest of his life. He went to bed sore all over and a little concerned about his future. All the animals lay on the ground facing Rufus. They all took turns watching him at night since they had never seen him so exhausted.

When morning came, the farmer and his wife were busy loading the buggy and feeding the animals. Although Rufus enjoyed making the children happy, he didn't think he had the strength to give rides for another half a day and then pull stumps for the other half. The farmer led Rufus to the buggy and hitched him up to it. Rufus was really surprised when the farmer and his wife tied Moocher and Uncle Spit Fire to the back. Not stopping there, they put Sparkle in a glass bowl and placed her on the front seat, and then they loaded up Quackers, Sonic Boom, and Fetch.

"Get along," the farmer told Rufus, who started pulling the buggy and all of his friends down the dusty, country road.

A mile down the road, the farmer made Rufus turn off and go toward the river. There, under a big oak tree, all the animals were let loose and Sparkle was placed on a wood crate so she could have a good view of everything. Rufus was untied and the farmer scratched him behind his ear and thanked him for all his hard work.

Rufus went and spent time with each of his friends and even let Quackers, Sonic Boom and Fetch ride on his back so he could show them how he entertained the little farmer children at the fair. It was the best day that the animals ever had in their whole lives and goodness and joy abounded.

The picnic in the shade was special indeed and the farmer's wife made sure to pack everybody's favorite foods. Because all the animals considered each other a part of their barnyard family, the picnic became known as the first barnyard family reunion.

Chapter Five: Copycat Mule

The next day, at exactly 6:30 a.m., the farmer came out and filled all the feed buckets with the animals' breakfast. Rufus was wondering if he was going to be worked again, but the farmer seemed to have other things on his mind and left as soon as he finished feeding us.

Rufus said, "Well, it looks as though I'll have to find something for myself to do in order to stay busy around here." He knew his options were going to be few and then an idea popped into his mule head. "I've got it," he said excitedly to himself. "I'll help all of my friends do their jobs."

Rufus trotted over to the water trough and asked me if I needed a hand. "Yes, I do," I said. "Could you pump the water handle so I can get more water to clean?"

"Sure," said Rufus excitedly. Rufus bit the handle to the water pump and wagged his head up and down causing water to pump out.

"Thank you, Rufus," I said.

"You're welcome, Sparkle," replied Rufus.

Rufus continued helping each of his friends until dinner came. They stopped to eat and then they played a few barnyard games until it was time to go to bed.

The Mule and the Thermometer

Chapter One: Home Sweet Home

"*Cock-a-doodle-doo,*" cried Sonic Boom, the rooster. "Okay, everybody, it's time to get up. Time for roll call, you sleepy heads," Sonic Boom continued. One-by-one the animals sounded back their presence when their names were called. Sonic Boom enjoyed going through the list of the animals' names for it gave him an important job in the morning. Going through the roll call list, he said, "Now, let me see here; we have Fetch the dog, Sparkle the goldfish."

"Here," I said back enthusiastically.

"Quackers the duck, Moocher the cow, Spit Fire the mule, and his nephew, Rufus — all present and accounted for," Sonic Boom said with a voice of satisfaction.

As the animals disbanded from roll call, the farmer made his way from the house out to the barn where he began to feed the animals.

"Here you go, old boy," the farmer said to Rufus as he poured some honey oats into his pail. Rufus gave out a loud donkey call to say, "Thank you," to the farmer and then he dipped his head in the pail and began to eat his breakfast. Rufus thought of all the starving little mules around the world. He imagined how bad life must be for other mules that didn't have the love that he was shown from the farmer. He knew that he was lucky to have the farmer as his friend because the farmer faithfully got up every morning and fed all of the farm animals and would spend time scratching Rufus behind the ear and talking to him.

"And here you go, my little lady," the farmer said to Sparkle as he added a few specks of fish food to the water trough. I popped the water with one of my fins to show my appreciation and then I ate breakfast even faster than Rufus was eating his.

The farmer pumped the water well a few times and filled the water trough full to the brim. He knew Sparkle liked it that way because it gave her more room to move around and it also raised her up high enough so she could peek over the edges and look around if she wanted to. As the farmer was pumping the well, he said to himself, "It appears the well is running dry because the water isn't coming out near as good as it normally does. It hasn't rained in months and the weather forecaster says it may not rain again for another month or so. I hope the well holds out, because I'd hate to lose you, Sparkle."

Rufus cried out in donkey language to the farmer, "What do you mean, 'lose Sparkle'?"

I interrupted Rufus and said, "He means that he will have to send me away to a place where there is more water if the well runs dry."

"What — send you away? For how long?" Rufus questioned more intently.

"It would be forever, Rufus. Once the farmer releases me into the lake, there will be no way to find me again," I said, trying to help Rufus deal with the possibility of having to let me go.

"No!" Rufus cried out as he heard my answer.

After learning of the possibility of losing me to the drought, Rufus stayed fixed to any news that he could learn concerning our weather conditions. Often, he trotted over to the farmer's house and listened to the radio in hopes that rain was on its way.

One day, the farmer came outside with a long glass stick with lots of markings on it. Rufus said to the farmer in mule language, "What is that for?"

After the farmer hung it on the wall, he pointed to the little marks on the glass tube and said, "Those are degree marks, Rufus. Every time the sun gets hotter on us, the mercury inside the thermometer will rise higher and higher. If it gets to here, it means it is dangerously hot outside and we should stay out of the heat as much as possible. And if the mercury gets below this mark then it is dangerously cold outside and means we need to be careful how long we are exposed to the cold."

"Wow," Rufus said to himself as he gave the farmer a big smile for showing him how to keep track of the weather at the very moment it was happening.

Rufus looked at the thermometer and said to himself, "Well, it's not dangerously hot, but it sure is close. I better go check up on my buddy, Sparkle, to see how she's doing."

Rufus walked over to my water trough and said, "Knock, knock, anybody home?"

I said, "Hi, Rufus, what brings you my way?"

"Hi, Sparkle," Rufus replied and then said, "I just learned how to tell how hot or cold it is outside by reading the farmer's thermometer."

"Really?" I asked in amazement. "I didn't know mules had such abilities."

Rufus nodded his head and continued, "Oh, yes, and although it isn't dangerously hot outside at the moment, the thermometer still shows that it is very hot outside and that we need to be careful how much sun we are getting."

"It does?" I questioned.

"Yes, it does," said Rufus. "And that is why I came over, so I could check up on you and see if you were all right."

"At the moment, I'm fine, Rufus, but the water is warmer than usual," I said, glad to know that my friends were looking after me.

"Okay then," Rufus said once more. "I'll go and keep my eyes and ears open on how the weather is going and will check up on you between weather reports."

"Thank you, Rufus," I said. "And come back any time, for you are always welcome at my home."

As Rufus left, I swam over to the shady part of the water trough in order to get out of the sun. The shade was twenty degrees cooler than it was in the sunny parts and the algae on the wall was soft as a feather bed. I took naps more often because the heat kept me exhausted.

Chapter Three: Desperate Measures

Another week passed and still no rain. Rufus said he heard on the news we were going through a drought. It was always good to learn new words that I could add to my vocabulary, but this word was a danger to our health.

The farmer and his wife were talking a lot more these last few days. They seemed bothered by the drought and it took up a great deal of their conversations.

"Rufus, my dear, would you pump some more water in the trough for me?" I asked

"Sure," Rufus said, always glad to do a good deed for someone else. "Up and down, up and down," Rufus sang as he pumped the handle up and down. It took a long time to fill the trough and Rufus and I realized that the well was almost dry and soon the farmer would be coming to remove me from the farm.

"If only I had a roof over my trough, I wouldn't lose so much water through evaporation."

"Evaporation?" Rufus inquired.

"It's the sun, Rufus," I said as I took a moment to teach him why my water kept disappearing. I continued my lecture by adding, "You see, Rufus, the heat from the sun's rays causes the water to turn into a very fine vapor, which rises into the air. The water will continue to steam up until there is no more water in the trough."

"No more water," Rufus cried out in donkey language, "but that'll kill you."

I tried to calm him down by saying, "I know, Rufus, and that is why before the trough runs dry, the farmer will take me away so I won't die."

"Oh," Rufus replied in a calmer tone, "what can we do to slow down evaporation?"

"Well, I suppose the only thing that we could do is block the sun with something," I answered.

Rufus thought for a moment and then bellowed out a loud mule call that alerted the other animals to come to the water trough for an emergency meeting.

"Rufus," I said. "What are you doing?"

"I'm calling for an emergency water trough meeting in order to find a way we can stop the water from evaporating," Rufus confidently said back to me.

"Quackers and I can hold out our wings and block the sun from shining directly on the water," Sonic Boom said with his piercing voice.

"That's great," Rufus said. "About how long can you hold out your wings?"

"About three minutes and then they are too heavy to lift," Quackers said joining the conversation.

"That will never help," replied Rufus.

Fetch barked out and then growled further by saying, "You will need something a lot bigger and stronger than you two if you are going to block the sun over the entire water trough."

"A lot bigger," Oinkers said from his pen across the road.

"I know," said Oinkers' wife, Snort. "What you need is really big, I mean mule big."

All of the animals slowly turned and faced Rufus.

"Very well, then," Rufus said as he turned toward his friends. "It's obvious that I must be the sun blocker, but I can't do this alone."

Quackers flew up on the pole next to Rufus and asked, "What do you need us to do?"

"What I need," Rufus said with a concerned tone in his voice, "is for all of you to promise that you won't splash water out of the trough or even drink from it. You must get your water from somewhere else, but not here where Sparkle lives. Agreed?"

All of the animals understood that Rufus was determined to keep Sparkle from being taken away from them so, in unison, they all nodded their heads as Sonic Boom shouted out, "Desperate times call for desperate measures; we'll do whatever it takes."

During the daylight hours, Rufus stood over the water trough keeping as much of the sun off Sparkle and her precious water as he could. Though this seemed to be a burden, Sparkle used the time to get to know Rufus better and to teach him whatever he was curious to learn about.

Rufus called out to Sonic Boom, "Where is the red mark on the thermometer?"

"It is even with the 103 mark," Sonic Boom cackled back.

Rufus was concerned because he was thirsty and losing a lot of his own water through perspiration.

"103 degrees," he said to himself, "and with four more hours to go."

"What's wrong?" I asked, looking up at Rufus.

"Um, nothing really," Rufus replied.

The farmer's wife came outside carrying with her an Easter hat and a pair of scissors. "Hi, Rufus," the farmer's wife said. Rufus gave her a soft mule huff and looked up at her. The farmer's wife began to cut the hat as she continued talking, "I see you are trying to block the sun with your body; that is why I came outside, so I could shape this hat so you can wear it. The hat will help keep the sun off your face and some of your body."

Rufus bellowed out a long mule greeting and asked, "How do I look in the hat?"

The farmer's wife giggled a little and then she reached up with her hands and held Rufus under his jaw while saying, "You are, without a doubt, the most handsome mule I've ever seen and with that hat on you look a lot like my husband."

As the farmer's wife was walking away, Rufus became excited at her compliment, to which he sang out his best mule song he could sing. "Did you guys hear that?" Rufus inquired. "She said I looked handsome," Rufus continued to brag to everyone.

Fetch decided he would have fun teasing Rufus about the hat, so he winked at the rest of the animals and then said, "It seems to me, Rufus, that you look more like a walking umbrella with hairy legs."

"No," Quackers interrupted, "Rufus looks more like a four-legged shade tree."

Sonic Boom decided he would play along, so he flew up on the edge of the water trough and said, "Actually, Rufus best resembles a parachute with four bony cords."

As the animals were laughing it up, I swam to the surface of the water and looked up toward everybody and asked, "Would y'all like to know what I see?"

"Sure," the animals said as they were still laughing at Rufus.

"I see a brave animal that is not afraid to sacrifice himself to save me," I said as the animals fell silent. I continued my speech by saying, "I see a true friend, whom I adore, who has been willing to allow himself to suffer all day long in this terrible heat, just to keep from losing me."

As I finished my speech, one-by-one the animals came up to Rufus with tears in their eyes and asked, "You know what, Sparkle? I see the same thing."

Rufus turned around to me as he softly said, "Thanks, Sparkle, for sticking up for me — you're a good friend to me."

I said back to Rufus, "Don't lose heart, my dear. We are all each other's good friends here; just sometimes we forget to show it."

Rufus smiled as he straightened himself up in a position of respectability. He was a sun blocker, which meant he had the most important job on the farm.

The next day, the farmer and his wife listened intently to the news. When it ended, they talked for some time before deciding to move Sparkle to the lake. The farmer and his wife came to the water trough carrying a pail and a fishnet.

"I'm sorry, Sparkle," the farmer said with a sad voice, "but it's time for you to go to your new home. The weatherman says it's not going to rain for at least another week and your water will all be gone by then."

Rufus began crying out in his native mule language as the farmer tried to push him away from the water trough. Rufus, unwilling to lose Sparkle, lowered his body onto the water trough and covered it completely.

"Well if that doesn't burn it all," the farmer said with true disappointment.

All the animals showed up and began squawking, quacking, and barking. Oinkers and Snort squealed as loudly as they could to help from across the road where they lived. The farmer was pushing Rufus from behind as his wife was tugging on Rufus's harness from the front.

"It's no use," the farmer's wife said. "This stubborn old mule has sat down and nothing is going to budge him now."

"You're right," the farmer said to his wife. "It looks like we'll have to come back later. Perhaps a few more days out in the sun will convince Rufus he needs to let us move Sparkle to the lake where there is plenty of water."

As the farmer and his wife left, the animals gathered around Rufus to celebrate their victory over keeping Sparkle from being moved to the lake.

Chapter Five: Good to Be Home

"*Cock-a-doodle-do,*" sounded Sonic Boom early the next morning. Sonic Boom followed his muster call with an important announcement, "Okay, guys and gals, due to the severe heat wave we are currently going through, exercise classes have been suspended until further notice."

Though the animals were glad that Sonic Boom was playing it safe by not making them exercise out in the heat, they all let him know how disappointed they were about the news.

Breakfast came right on time, as it did every morning. The farmer loved the animals as though they were his own children. Because the farmer truly cared for his animals, he was happy to take good care of them by making sure they ate right every day. I got a nice big smile and a few sprinkles of fish food, Rufus got hay and oats, Fetch got dry dog food and a ham bone, Sonic Boom and Quackers got fed a mixture of seeds and pellet, while Oinkers and Snort got table scraps the farmer jokingly called pig slop.

As everybody was eating, the farmer and his wife came over to me and scooped me out of my trough and placed me inside a pail of water. Before the other animals knew what was going on, I was on the front seat of the pickup truck. When Rufus realized what was going on, he tried opening the gate so he could bring me back but couldn't because the farmer had locked the gate.

As the farmer and his wife headed down the dusty road toward the lake, Rufus and the other animals cried out to me their love and devotion. All I could do was reassure everyone in tears that we would see each other again some day. I was terrified of being released into the lake, for it was equivalent to an ocean when compared to how small I was. I knew deep down in my heart that if I were released in the lake, I would never see my friends again.

The farmer's wife was crying along with me and as she cried, she reached over and took her husband by the hand, saying, "My dearest, is there nothing else we can do to save Sparkle?"

The farmer looked at his wife with compassion as he realized that losing even the smallest of their animals would be too hard for them to bear.

As I was looking out through the windows of the pickup truck, I noticed that we passed the road that pointed to the lake.

The farmer turned to his wife and with a big smile on his face said, "My dearest, I think I have a solution to Sparkle's problem."

The farmer and his wife went to the pet store where they bought all kinds of pretty things. They raced home and quickly rushed everything and me inside the house. At the dining room window that faced the pen and water trough, the farmer and his wife began putting together their newly purchased items. They filled it with water and lowered the curtain to hide it. Then, they brought Rufus and the other animals over to the window for the surprise show. As the animals stood facing the window, the curtain was slowly raised.

As I came into their view, I cried out, "Surprise! Welcome to my new glass water trough."

No longer did Rufus have to suffer trying to keep the sun off me because I was inside the shady house with the farmer and his wife. My fish tank had a large variety of pretty rocks and toy divers and even a treasure chest with bubbles coming out of it that gave really good massages. When my farm friends saw me, they all erupted into joyful animal sounds. From that day on, anytime one of the animals wanted to visit me, all they had to do was walk over to the window where I moved to.

The farmer placed the thermometer close to the fish tank, so that everyone could see just how hot it was getting. Weeks passed before the rains finally came, but after the first few inches had fallen, the farmer took me back to the trough where he knew I really wanted to be. Once again, I was close to my friends and this time for good.

Rufus came up to me and said, "I'm so glad you're back home in the pen with the rest of us, Sparkle."

Although it was strange moving back to my old home, I felt so relieved and comforted in being there once again. I looked up at all my wonderful farmyard friends and said, "It's good to be home."

Story Tree

Chapter One: The Adolescent Historian

During summer vacation, I generally spend most of my time out in the backyard. Growing there is the grandest of all trees in my hometown. No other tree for miles around could compare to its massive size and strength. My tree almost covers the entire back yard and goes up so high that I get dizzy just trying to see its top. For a tree to be this huge, it must have been growing for a long, long time.

Me? Well, you could say I've been around a long time also, because I remember when Mrs. Crumble's hen house blew over and all her birds were running around loose for several weeks. The cats really had a great time hunting them, but let me inform you that a scared chicken can fly. I didn't know what was noisier, the chickens clucking or Mrs. Crumble squawking about her poor chickens. I also remember when the Second Street fire main sprayed water straight up like a super-sized water fountain after Snider Johnson ran over it with his hot rod convertible. I also lived through the coldest winter that was ever recorded in Rigley County.

The giant tree I was bragging about earlier was what I considered as my home away from home.

I laboriously built a tree house between its branches using the scrap lumber that we had behind the tool shed. Although it took months to complete, it was by far the best place on earth that anyone could hope for. The tree was the perfect escape away from home and yet it was still close enough to the back door just in case I had to use the bathroom. I was proud to be a homeowner, even if it was up a tree. I'm not even close to the smartest kid out there, but I'm sure an adult elephant could live inside my tree house without breaking a limb.

Chapter Two: Stranger in My Own Backyard

One day when I was in my tree house, I pondered the age of the tree and all that must have happened around it. I could just imagine the tales this tree could tell if only it could talk. The tree was not only good for goofing around in, but it was especially good for taking naps. As I lay my head down on one of the cushions that I borrowed from one of our lawn chairs, my body drifted off in sleep while my thoughts stayed firmly fixed on the old tree and what it must have endured to have survived such a long time.

When I awoke from my nap, everything that was once my home and community was gone; even my tree house had vanished and the tree that I was in was very small compared to the one that is in my backyard.

Looking out through the branches, I could see a vast prairie surrounding me. Before I could begin to get upset about my situation, a storm began developing over my head. The clouds soon made everything dark as night and cool as the first winter weather when it rushes in. Thunder began clattering out as lightning bolts shot across the sky. One bolt of lightning struck the ground miles away at the horizon and a great wall of smoke soon formed and began blowing in my direction. There was a deafening rumble and the ground seemed to shake and within a minute, thousands of buffalo came running in my direction. I was terrified as I clung to the tree. One great impact after another came to the tree as each out-of-control beast slammed into it. Just as soon as the herd of buffalo passed by, a heavy and unrelenting rain began pouring down upon me. The rain extinguished the fire, but the water was flowing dangerously fast. It swept underneath me and I cried for fear that it would sweep the tree away, which was my only protection from the mudslide. The roots were deep and the tree held its ground. The clouds emptied their watery cargo onto the soaked, sponge-like earth and the storm finally passed with the tree standing taller and prouder, having overcome this great test of endurance against the elements of nature. The tree took its bounty from the storm as it drank in the rain that was left behind. Its roots held as much water as they could, for it instinctively knew there was no guarantee that rain would come any time soon. I suppose the tree was glad, but I was soaking wet and miserable. I was fully convinced that I was not about to climb down from this tree, for it had already saved me from being trampled and drowned.

Chapter Three: The Unstoppable Force

I could hear the clattering of metal and wood creaking as an old western wagon team approached. Through the leaves, I saw the driver pull on the reins as he said, "Whoa, now, whoa." As the wagon came to a stop near the tree I was in, a pioneer family climbed out and began making a place for a picnic.

I didn't make a noise as I continued watching them. One of the men pulled an ax out of a side chest and asked the elderly man, "Do you want me to cut the tree down to get what fire wood we can out of it?"

The elderly man looked around for a moment of reflection and then answered, "No, not this one." The elderly man knew that the wood from the tree was green and would cause too much smoke if used for cooking fuel. Wisdom seemed to overshadow his entire composure and I suspect the real reason he didn't want to cut the tree down was because it was the only shade for miles in any direction.

As the younger man began putting the ax away, he replied, "Just as well, Mr. Rigley; there are plenty of dried buffalo chips lying about to last us for years."

The women spread a heavy wool blanket on the ground just under the shade and placed a basket in the middle. The people circled the basket and held hands with the person who stood next to them. All the men and boys had already removed their hats and they all bowed their heads as the elderly man said, "Let us give thanks." The man was so sincere in all that he said about the safety of their trip, their good health, and the abundance of food that they had to eat. When the old man finished speaking, they all sat down and ate a very meager meal. I couldn't actually see what they were so thankful for because all they had was some tough jerky, stale bread, beans, and some peach preserves. Although I saw very little, they believed they were blessed. In all that they did, they did it with manners and gentleness toward each other. It made me homesick for the times when I was asked to say the blessing over our meals.

I began to realize just how good life had always been for me at home, with the abundance of different kinds of foods we had stored in our refrigerator. They didn't have tea, milk, juice, colas, or any of the hundreds of things we ate and drank. All they had was water and it didn't come with flavors or ice, but was dipped out of a barrel that was attached to the side of the wagon. These humble people were so grateful and yet they actually had so little. I, on the other hand, have so much yet I'm always trying to escape from it to my tree house or to hang out with one of my friends. I couldn't wait for my chance to go home and start showing my parents just how grateful I am for their love and all the hard work they do so I can have so much.

The pioneers packed and rode off and just as soon as they were out of sight, I noticed balls of smoke rising up from the tops of three mountain ridges. As the smoke melted away, I noticed riders heading for the tree. Two riders arrived first and they remained seated on their horses until the others arrived. One was the leader and the other a guard. The leader raised his hand in greeting to the other leaders, and then they dismounted their horses. The three chiefs sat just below me in the shade as the three guards stood off a short distance, allowing the horses to feed on prairie grass. As the chiefs finished their discussion, they shared a pipe together and then headed off to where they came from.

No sooner had the Indians gone than a dust cloud over the distant trail bellowed up. In front of the dust came a large company of cavalry troops who came to a halt right before me. Their uniforms were so dusty that I couldn't tell what color was underneath. One soldier was an Indian who wore a soldier's jacket. He examined the ground where the three chiefs sat earlier, then reported his findings to their commander. He gave a salute and then mounted his horse. The second rider from the front yelled with a loud voice, "Forward," and the entire company rode off.

Chapter Four: There Is No Place Like Home

As the day wore on, I saw the vast expanse of history that surrounded the tree that I used as my home away from home. At each event, the tree seemed to gain a little more size. With all that I had been through, I was really worn down and needed to take a nap. Without any further disturbances, I closed my eyes for the slumber of a lifetime. Sleep is so unfair, it seems, for just as soon as I had closed my eyes, I was opening them once again. There was no telling just how long I had been asleep, but it only seemed like seconds.

I awoke to the voice of my dad calling for me from the back door of our house. He said I needed to come in and get cleaned up for supper because Mom had made my favorite meal. I sure liked it when my mom did those kinds of things for us. I also liked it when either of my parents would spend time with me in the backyard playing, wrestling, or tossing the ball.

I climbed down the tree imitating how a squirrel would do it and wouldn't you know, I slipped and fell on my head. But landing on my head was okay, because it was fun and it didn't hurt that much. As I reached the door, I glanced back for another look at my favorite tree in Rigley County. It looked so different to me now, and no matter how old I was when I returned home, I would take time to go out to the backyard and sit for a spell in my tree house and reflect on all the important lessons I learned from this amazing story tree.

The House

Chapter One: They Say

There it is again, that same old creepy house that rests on Carver's Ridge. The house has always been an unsolvable mystery to me, but I think the owner must have been insane to have purposefully built his Victorian mansion right next to Indian Peak Cemetery. Indian Peak is the mountain our small community of Miner's Junction is located on. Still, though, I'd like to know why anyone would build a house next to a graveyard and as ghastly as they both looked together, I have no doubts that the people who once lived in the house are now the ones whose names appear upon the tombstones nearby. No one could have found two places of equal spookiness, for both seem to say together when you look upon them, *Keep out*, *No trespassing*, or *Enter at your own risk*. Either way, I still have to see that creepy old house and its ghostly graveyard every time we go to town. As I continued pondering how unlikable the house was to me, the trees blocked it from my view as the car made its way to our own home. My thoughts gave me the uneasy feeling that there were eyes looking back at me from somewhere within the house.

After dinner, we listened to the radio and then Papa read a portion of the Bible to us, as he did every night before we went to bed. We especially liked hearing the stories of the many people who got healed from all their sicknesses. When Papa finished reading to us, he told us to get ourselves cleaned and ready for bed. We did exactly what Papa said, for we knew he would not tolerate our disobedience and that he was quick to respond if we failed to mind him. Mom didn't like disobedience either because getting into trouble meant there was strife in the family and that was something she would not tolerate. She was just as firm-handed as Papa was with her expectations of us minding and being helpful. Mom was petite and she rarely raised her voice, but if she ever had to punish us, she would make sure that we never forgot her skill with a peach switch. She was always looking out for our best interest, especially our best interest in doing chores around the house.

"Good night, Mama, good night, Papa," I said, as I hugged and kissed each one of my parents on the cheek.

"Good night, sweetheart," was their reply.

My little brother, Tommy, followed my routine of hugging and kissing our parents and saying his good nights for it was soon to be lights out and eyes closed.

Tommy was a few inches shorter than me and that was probably due to the fact that he was a year younger. I often teased him by telling him that he was adopted just so I could watch him squeal like a pig. We both looked so much alike in the face, though, that people often mistook us as twins. Papa didn't worry about who was who, because when he gave an order, we both tore into action like a couple of hound dogs fighting over a fresh stew bone under the house.

As we were lying in bed, Tommy was busy jacking his jaw about some story he heard concerning the old house on Carver's Ridge. He said that it used to be owned by an old Civil War general by the name of Randal Scott McClennon. Supposedly, back in the old days, it was one of the most beautiful mansions that had ever been built. The general was well-known because he had a regular stream of visitors coming and going throughout the many years that he lived there. The more Tommy talked, the more I was convinced that he had fallen prey to some more trash talk, which constantly overflowed from Bob Parson's imagination. Bob carried the unofficial title of being the biggest storyteller in Lawrence County. Unfortunately for me, my little brother believed every word that galloped full speed out of Bob's mouth. And now it was about something I didn't even like to think about, which was the possibility of having to go inside the spooky, old house.

I was about to frog Tommy in the arm in an attempt to shut him up, but he dodged my punches long enough to beg me to give him a chance to tell the rest of the story. When he mentioned gold bars and how finding it could really help our parents out, I decided to go back to my bed and give him one last chance to convince me. He said that the old house was also known as the McClennon Mansion, because it was named after the original owner. McClennon, they say, was a Civil War veteran with so many medals that he almost made General MacArthur look like a cub scout by comparison. Apparently, at the end of the war, McClennon saw his efforts to free the Confederacy from Yankee control burning to the ground in ashes. When he received orders from General Lee to surrender his forces to the northern army, he felt betrayed and humiliated by his commanders. Government investigators at that time believed that just before the war ended, McClennon found his chance to get reimbursed for his efforts by robbing the last gold shipment that was headed up to Richmond. With help from soldiers who were still loyal to his command, they seized the rail car that carried the last of the Confederacy's gold. He afterwards lived out the rest of his life at the mansion and nobody ever discovered what happened to the money or the men who were last seen with McClennon. The military tried to convict him of several crimes, but failed in their attempts due to the lack of evidence and witnesses. It is said that McClennon got rid of the men who helped him rob the train by holding a banquet in their honor. As they toasted their glasses they swallowed to their deaths the poison that tainted their drinks. The graveyard provided McClennon a handy way to dispose of his victims. Years later, when his time came to die, he chose to take with him the secret to the whereabouts of the gold. He was buried at Indian Peek Cemetery and shortly afterward his house was seized and searched from top to bottom without the investigators finding the gold they were hoping to recover. Unwilling to waste any more time searching for the stolen gold, the government had his personal items shipped to his next of kin and the windows were boarded up and the doors locked for good, in order to keep people away from the house.

They say that McClennon's spirit stayed behind to haunt those who came looking for his hidden treasure. They also say that if anyone could remain there one full night, then he would reward them by telling them where he hid his ill-gotten gold. To this day, no one has dared to go inside the house.

When Tommy finished his story, I jumped out of my bed and stated, "Papa says there are no such things as ghosts and if there is gold to be found, then us Sutton boys will be the ones to find it, for we aren't scared of nothing." The issue was settled as far as Tommy and I were concerned and when the time was right, we would be off looking for gold bars that had to be somewhere inside the house.

Tommy and I slugged each other in the arm to prove our toughness to each other and then we jumped into our beds. My thoughts were full of hope about the chance we had at becoming rich because no one had ever found the hidden gold. As I lay there feeling the sting from Tommy's punch, I drifted off to sleep dreaming of our plans and where to look once we were inside the house.

Chapter Two: Mission in the Making

October 31 was the day that we decided would be our best shot at looking for the gold. Tommy and I had been planning this day for a long time and tonight we would finally get our chance to perform our covert operation. If anyone were to see us walking down the road, they would naturally assume that we were out trick-or-treating and not up to mischief. Our plan was flawless and that is because Sutton boys tend to be natural born geniuses. Either way, in the back of my mind, I knew that it would take a good deal of imagination to find the missing gold that was hidden somewhere inside the house.

At school, the classroom was filled with kids who were coughing because they had just come in from playing outside in the cool mountain air. When the teacher had her back turned toward us, Tommy and I passed notes to each other. Lucky for us, she didn't see what we were doing or we would had been in serious trouble and our plans ruined for recovering the missing gold that was sure to be somewhere within the house.

After school let out, Tommy and I hurried home in hopes of gaining the extra time we would need to prepare our gear for the mission. Though Mom didn't own a piano, she often went into town in order to practice on the one the church had. After she finished practicing, she would always sit on the shaded park bench and wait for Papa to drive by and pick her up. If Papa was running a little late from the mining company, she would make good use of the time by talking to those who passed by. I think she liked it when Papa was running late, because it gave her more time to socialize with the many good people who lived in Miner's Junction. Little did she or anybody else know that tonight Tommy and I would be trick-or-treating our way into bars of gold that were waiting for us to dig up somewhere in the old, abandoned house.

We borrowed from the tool shed a spare miner's lantern and two shovels. We also found a few candles and a box of matches. We took our gear and hid everything in Papa's rundown Model-T pickup that was parked at the front corner of our driveway. Returning from the truck to our rooms, we got our grubby clothes ready to wear. We knew that digging for gold would get us dirty, so we weren't taking any chances by messing up our good clothes. One thing our mother would surely switch us for was messing up good clothes when work clothes could have been used. Our plans were rock solid and all our gear was hidden and ready for action. The only thing that remained was waiting for our parents to fall asleep so we could sneak out. Tonight, Tommy and I would prove that there was no ghost and that the missing gold was hidden all along, somewhere inside the old house.

Because we weren't allowed to practice Halloween, we went to bed early as usual. We ate, listened to the radio, had our story time, got cleaned up, and then said our goodnights. About an hour after we were in bed, we heard our parents' bedroom door close. No sooner had the door closed than Tommy and I were dressed and outside, running down the driveway, and heading toward the pickup truck. Not knowing if our parents would wake up in the middle of the night, we left them a note on our bunk that explained why we weren't home. The note would keep them from thinking we had run away, but that we could be found somewhere inside the old house.

Chapter Three: Covert Operation

As we were walking down the road, we realized that it would have been wiser if we had worn our jackets and not used shoes that had holes in them. When we arrived at Indian Peak Cemetery, we saw the giant outline of the mansion just beyond it. Though we could have taken the long path around the graveyard to avoid any of its many tripping hazards, the cold air pressured us to take the short cut through it. About halfway through the graveyard, I realized for the first time that Sutton boys could become scared of certain things. Although I wasn't too keen on touching my brother — unless it was to frog him in the arm — I was glad we were shoulder to shoulder as we pressed on. Suddenly, an owl hooted and that was all the encouragement we needed to cut and run. We ran wide-eyed and didn't stop until we were standing in the very presence of the gloomy, old house.

Our leg muscles felt like they were about to explode and our lungs gulped down air like a starving man does food. Just as soon as we caught our breaths, Tommy asked, "Do you think we should go inside or should we do this some other time?" He was chickening out and I could tell it in his voice. With a stern voice I replied, "Look here, I didn't come this far just to see us give up." Tommy's disappointment was obvious, but he nodded his head to let me know I could count on him. We had no choice but to make our way up the porch slowly, because every board seemed to moan in agony when we stepped on them. One thing for sure, if I were in as bad a shape as this old place was, I'd make all kinds of funny noises to prove it. The front doors were massive and they creaked so badly when we open them that my teeth wanted to shatter. The lantern was steadily losing light power, which meant that its fuel supply was running low. Though we preferred the lantern, we remembered bringing candles and so we pressed onward, ever further inside the old house.

Just beyond the front door was a grand staircase. Next to it was a door that led into a large parlor. Above the parlor's fireplace was a dusty painting of the general himself. He was sitting in a chair with a sword across his lap and he had one of his hands stuck halfway inside the chest of his uniform coat. As I was admiring the general's portrait, there was a tremendous explosion as the front door closed violently. Tommy and I dashed back to the door, with our minds becoming desperate as we struggled to reopen it. From within one of the rooms at the top of the staircase, we heard a horrible scream. Then a high-pitched voice shouted out saying, "Run or die, Yankees!" We practically jumped out of our skin as we both yelled and ran for the closest door that would open up to us. Down the hallway, we found a door that would open and without a second thought, we took it. Terrified from what was happening, we sprang down the stairs not fully realizing that it went to the cellar, which led us further into the bowels of the haunted house.

Once again we heard the terrible voice as it screamed out its warning, "Run or die, Yankees!" When we reached the back wall of the cellar, the lantern started to burn out, so we quickly lit our candles and placed them in front of our dead-end position. I grabbed my shovel and held it like I was ready to knock a home run. Tommy was almost in shock and was leaning against the wall staring wide-eyed in disbelief at the eerie form that was coming toward us, deep within the house.

Chapter Four: That Was a Good One

As we stood there waiting to see what would happen next, we heard in the distance the tune of *Dixie Land* being whistled. As the sound drew closer, we could make out the sound of footsteps slowly making their way down the stairwell. The form stopped just within the cover of the darkness and so I frantically called to Tommy to help me fight for our lives. Laughter followed the song and instantly I knew this was no ghost to fear, but a prankster to hurt. "Bob Parsons, is that you?" I asked. Sure enough, Bob stepped into the light as he continued to laugh us to shame. I was thinking of pounding the daylights out of Bob, but I was truly glad that it was him and not McClennon's ghost. It was a huge embarrassment and I knew that at school the joke would live on and on. A smile started to form on my face as I began to realize just how big Bob's joke really was. Tommy and I joined in and all of us were laughing in the cellar of the house.

After our long, relieving laugh, I said, "That was a good one." I proceeded to asked Bob how he knew we would be here on this particular night and he said he saw us passing notes in class and volunteered to help the teacher clean up after school so he could go through the trash and read them. I turned and looked at Tommy and decided not to slug him in the arm because we both were guilty of being careless. I confessed to Bob that I felt like a blue ribbon fool by falling for the world's biggest shuck-and-jive ever invented. He listened with complete satisfaction and pride for a job well done. Tommy asked Bob where he came up with the story of the stolen gold and he said the story was actually true. He learned about it one night from his uncle when he came over for a visit. It was a true moment of mixed emotions for I actually wanted to talk to Bob about his trick he pulled on us, yet I also wanted to get out of the basement and away from this worthless, old house.

Chapter Five: Luck of the Leprechaun

The candles would soon be used up, so I told Tommy to get me one of the torches that still hung on the wall. As he pulled the torch, a deep mechanical sound was heard coming through the wall and there, to our surprise, was a seam that ran from the ceiling to the ground. We lit the torch where it was and jammed our shovel into the seam. On the count of three, we pushed with all we had and the wall swung open. Inside the secret room, we found a mound of stacked gold bars and several bags filled with Confederate bills and coins. We each grabbed some money to prove our stories and then left that wonderfully forsaken house.

Months passed before we received the reward money for making the discovery. Papa spent some of the money on paying off the rest of our home loan. He also bought our mom a bunch of new dresses and her very own piano. Papa spent some of the money to get his old Model-T running again. Tommy and I got new clothes, athletic gear, and the peach switch from Mama. Papa also grounded us for a whole month in order to help us remember that we weren't supposed to do things behind their backs. He said that we had the luck of the leprechauns on our side the night we found the gold. He went on to explain just how dangerous it was, because there might have been an escaped felon hiding out somewhere inside the old house.

One night, vandals set the McClennon mansion on fire. The wood was so dry that it burned to the ground in less than an hour. Only then did I understand what Papa meant about the dangers of sneaking off, with no one knowing that we had foolishly entered the house.

Miracle Lake

Chapter One: Just Another Fishing Trip

"Come on, Jimmy, or you'll be late to catch all the good fish," I cried out from the pickup truck.

Jimmy said, "Okay, Grandpa," then he ran and jumped into the pickup truck and crawled over my lap and to his seat.

I leaned over and kissed the top of Jimmy's head as I held him for a moment. I was thankful for every moment I got to spend with my grandson, because of the terrible price paid to have him live with Edna and myself. Both of Jimmy's parents were killed in an auto accident when he was only three and lucky for us, Jimmy was staying over for the weekend when they had their wreck. The thought of losing all three of them made me shutter every time it crossed my mind. As I was giving Jimmy the usual long hug that he got every time we went somewhere, I said in a scolding tone in my inner voice, "You have two of mine already, God, but I refuse to let you have this one."

"The drive to the lake is pleasant today, Jimmy," I said in order to start a conversation.

Jimmy, being completely absorbed in his reel, nodded his head and said, "Yep."

I continued my attempt to talk with Jimmy by describing what could be seen if he would only turn his eyes toward the window.

"Sure is a bright enough day out today."

"Yep," Jimmy continued to say.

"Look at the grain fields dance from the wind pushing them along." I invited Jimmy to be involved with the world around him. I realized that I had gotten onto the wrong topic and changed it to the reason for our trip.

"Jimmy, my boy, we have to get to the lake as soon as the daylight starts, because if we wait too long then the fish will go bad on us."

Jimmy asked curiously back, "Grandpa, what is the difference between good fish and bad fish, anyway?"

"Well, son," I replied, "the good fish are the ones that wake up hungry and ready to strike at anything that we cast at them, while the bad fish are those who have already had their breakfast and are no longer hungry. The good fish and the bad fish are the same fish; I just call them bad if they no longer want to eat, but only want to play follow the leader."

"Oh," said Jimmy, "so when Grandma chooses not to eat with us, because she is counting her calories, then she is being a bad grandma, right?"

"Well, not exactly, son," responded Grandpa with a smile on his face, "though she may not always eat when we do, she sure likes it when I catch her in my arms and tell her how wonderful she is to have."

Jimmy seemed to like my answer, because after hearing it he burst out laughing. I was soon laughing along with him, and the rest of the drive to the lake was one chuckle after another.

Chapter Two: S.O.S.

The lake was in perfect form when we arrived and the water had a deep ocean blue that sparkled from thousands of flashes of reflected sunlight. The ducks were entertaining us with their diving and landing skills and shade graced the grassy banks all along the lake. With all these wonders, it was the cool breeze that made being there so right. The wind gently blew its coldness against our skin and was invigorating and calming. The cool breeze and the constant falling of leaves served to remind us that winter wasn't too far away. Though many in our community did not like the freezing winters that came every year, the changes in our seasons were always met with expectation and awe.

Jimmy and I sat down on the old but sturdy wooden pier, hanging our legs over the edge of its boardwalk. With synchronized precision, we both cast our lines out in hopes of being the one who got the first fish of the day. It was said to be good luck to catch the first fish, which motivated our first competitive challenge between us.

Being the grandfather of our fishing brigade, I automatically held the prestigious office of Inquisitive Child Answering Technician. No sooner had our corks hit the water when my audacious eight-year-old companion asked his question.

Jimmy inquired, "Grandpa, why do we call it fishing when we use poles and hooks instead of fish to catch fish?"

"I'm not sure, Jimmy," I said back with a concerned look on my face, "but I do understand why you wonder about it." After a few moments of serious reflection, I raised one of my eyebrows and said, "I wonder what we ought to call fishing if not fishing? Perhaps you could help the world solve this great problem by thinking of a suitable name."

Jimmy thought for a moment and then, lifting one of his own eyebrows in order to imitate me, he said, "I suppose we should call fishing what it really is."

"And what is that?" I asked back.

Jimmy said with a triumphant smile, "Fishing should be called hooking."

I was amazed at the answer as I responded back to him, "Good name to call it, Jimmy, because I have hooked more than fish in these waters over the years."

"I wish Grandma would have come with us this time," Jimmy said disappointingly.

I said, "I totally agree, Jimmy; it would have been better if Grandma would have helped us do some of this hooking." I then changed the subject and asked, "You want to know what I think?"

"Tell me, Grandpa, what is it?" Jimmy asked curiously.

"I bet you first picks," I continued saying, "that Grandma Edna is home right now baking us a batch of her yummy oatmeal raisin cookies in the oven."

To that, Jimmy squirmed, squealed, and licked his lips as though he could actually taste the cookies.

"Jimmy, you've got one," was all that I could say as I watched his fishing pole bend from something heavy. As I helped Jimmy lift his rod out of the water, up jumped the biggest freshwater bass I'd ever seen. It must have been ten pounds and I must have been close to having a heart attack from the shock of the catch and all the excitement that was going on.

Jimmy was jumping up and down shouting, "Yippy, I got the first catch! I got the first catch!"

I grabbed the fish and tried to pull the hook out of its mouth and found that it was set hard in its jaw. I reached for my pliers because it would be impossible to remove the hook without them and realized I didn't bring them with me.

"Uh oh, Jimmy," I said like the class dunce, "I forgot my pliers in the glove box and have to go back to the truck to get them, so just stay where you are and I will be back in a flash."

As I hurried back to the truck, I could hear Jimmy shouting, "Okay, Grandpa, but you better get a move on it because this fish is mad and is trying to get loose."

As I reached the truck, I heard a splash and glanced back but couldn't see Jimmy anywhere. Terror struck my mind as I began running and screaming for Jimmy. "Jimmy!" I shouted over and over as I ran back to the pier. I ran as fast as this old man could and when I reached the pier, Jimmy was nowhere to be seen. There was a fresh blood stain on the boat that was tied up to the pier. It became obvious to me what happened and without shedding one stitch of clothing, I immediately jumped into the lake to rescue Jimmy. As I reached the bottom, there to my worst nightmare was the motionless body of my beloved grandson. As my head came out of the water I began shouting, "Jimmy, breathe!" The people who owned the boat had heard my cries and came running from where they were. I struggled to reach the shore, for I had little strength left from all the running and swimming I had just done. I could barely breathe myself, but did what I could for Jimmy until the couple arrived and took over. They tried frantically to perform CPR, but stopped when they noticed the bloody wound to Jimmy's head. I lost my composure and sobbed out my plea, "No, dear God in Heaven, don't let this boy be dead." The couple had a radio in the boat and called for emergency assistance. I collapsed in anguish next to my precious grandson, Jimmy, wrapping my arms around him in hopes that life would somehow return to him.

Chapter Three: Hook, Line, and Sinker

Edna and I laid Jimmy to rest between both of his parents. My body is weak and my will to go on with life has left me. I carry around my soul the heavy chains of guilt that were made by my foolish mistake, which cost my grandson his life. My mind is haunted with the images of that day. My conscience won't allow me rest from thinking of how I left a small boy by himself on a fishing pier. At night, I have trouble sleeping; only through exhaustion does rest finally come. My wife is concerned for me and she is lost for words that would comfort me. Everything leads back to my guilt concerning Jimmy's death, but even though she never says it, deep down in her heart she knows that I'm at fault. She notices I'm withdrawn and does what she can to encourage me to eat and move around.

One night, as I was finally calming down and finally giving my body over to rest, I was suddenly aroused by a brilliant light that had warmth to it. As I stared at it, a voice spoke these words so tenderly to me, "Go to the lake tonight and receive a miracle." I jumped out of bed and began putting on my robe. My wife, Edna, was doing the same as she exclaimed that she also saw and heard the vision and was going with me. Neither of us doubted that something supernatural was happening and that we were suppose to obey the vision. Nothing in this world, not even the harsh winter weather, was going to keep us from visiting the lake tonight.

Chapter Four: The One That Got Away

It was very cold that night and the drive was longer than usual, for winter always showed its presence here with lots of snow and cold wind. As we arrived at the lake, we both got out and started to walk toward the pier where Jimmy was last seen alive. All of a sudden, the clouds exploded with great ferocity. Lightning bolts were flashing all across the sky as thunder joined the heavenly display. It was the most terrible storm I'd ever seen and it was happening all around us. Then without any natural reason, the storm suddenly stopped. As we stood there shivering and embracing each other, the clouds split open and a very bright light showed through. As we stared up at the light, the same voice that we had heard in our bedroom was tenderly speaking to us once more saying, "Fear not, for I have heard your cries of anguish and have felt the burden of guilt that tears at your soul. Be comforted in knowing that this night has been set aside for you."

The clouds melted away and the whole lake area was ablaze with mid-day light. The snow that covered everything in a heavy blanket of white perfection began to rapidly melt as grass came out and took its place. Flowers bloomed and the trees came to full shade in a matter of minutes. It was springtime in the dead of winter and as we turned marveling at all the lush beauty, we froze in a near panic when we saw our little grandson, Jimmy, standing before us with his arms outstretched. There he was very much alive and standing between both of his parents, who had been dead for the past five years. I fell to my knees as little Jimmy came running up to me. It was the longest hug I had ever given anyone. As the tears came gushing out of my eyes, I burst into laughter and a joyful chant, "My boy, my dear, sweet boy, you are alive and well!" Edna was busy hugging and kissing Jimmy's parents. We were on an emotional roller coaster as we found ourselves both laughing and crying at the same time.

Winter began to slowly creep back into the landscape, and we knew that the time that was given us would soon end. I knelt before Jimmy and held him in my arms. As I was begging his forgiveness, he stopped me and said, "Grandpa, don't cry anymore and don't feel bad for me or for what happened that day at the pier. I have no reason to forgive you for anything, for you loved me with all your heart and even prayed that day that God would not allow me to die. My parents and I know you love me, and what is most important, God knows your heart is pure and that you would have never purposefully hurt me. You only wanted what was best for me. My death — like my parents' — was an accident. I am home now with my parents and that is all that matters between us. So please don't cry any longer for me, for I am not dead, but in a better world. Now, give me one more hug and kiss for it is time for us to return to heaven." And so with one last embrace, our precious children disappeared in the light. There was only one thing that Edna and I felt we had to do before we left and that was to fall upon our knees and give thanks to the Lord.

Chapter Five: The Lake Record

That Sunday morning, I entered the church and though they were in the middle of a worship song, the music stopped as everyone turned and greeted me. News in a community the size of ours traveled quickly, but the content of what took place had it moving at the speed of light.

As soon as Edna and I had taken a seat, Pastor Murphy called to me and said, "Brother Sam, we are so glad to have you back after your long absence from us. We hear from others that you have some good news; would you be so kind as to share it with us and give us a first-hand account of the happenings that you witnessed at the lake?"

"I'd be glad to tell you what the Lord has done in our lives," I replied back as Edna was gently squeezing my hands to offer me her support.

Mayor Dupree and Joe Newman from the city counsel were in the audience, along with Noreen Burks, who was the county's newspaper columnist.

I started my message by saying, "I set the lake record a few days ago, by reeling in the biggest miracle one could ever hope to catch." The people were awestruck by the message and, as they listened, every face was radiant with joy and hope of the glory promised them.

The story was first printed in the local papers, but the excitement caused an unstoppable momentum that caused the miracle story to be printed in the largest media outlets all across the nation. The mayor called for a special city counsel meeting and it seemed as though the entire town turned out for it. The chamber room was also packed with TV cameras and newspaper reporters and within the space of half an hour, Superior Lake had officially been changed to Miracle Lake. Even before the meeting was announced to the public, the mayor had already ordered the replacement signs to be made ready for installation at a moment's notice. During the meeting, the maintenance crews were in position, standing by their radios, waiting to get the go-ahead to replace the old signs with the new ones. But they weren't the only things that got changed that day, for many people's hearts were also changed. I believe that the story of Miracle Lake generated a new devotion within the lives of many people whose hopes had once been destroyed through their many hardships and failed expectations. Even I, the grandpa who became so bitter toward God and so discouraged about life, could only look forward to the great family reunion he has promised to all of those who truly love him and who diligently seek his face.

The Legend of the Turkey

Many moons ago, in the ancient land of *Ameri-cani-shash-shin-onne*, there lived the tribal people of the *Mani-woo-ku-wok-kinosse*. They were a kind and peace-loving folk who respected all life. They were the guardians of this ancient land, whom the Great Spirit, *Pawn-nay-leeki-taw-neh-nicco*, blessed with many flowing rivers of pure waters, towering, dark forest of endless evergreens, and expansive lush grasslands that fed many buffalo and deer.

It was in the village of *Trawco-layhont-onno-vina* that lived the wisest man of all the people. Every young brave would have to come and learn from him concerning the mysteries of life. The wise man's name was *Low-kay-dena-law-cheh-nenna*. His name was spoken affectionately and with great respect and it was required of all the young braves to visit his teepee before being initiated into manhood.

It was in this setting that the lads found themselves before the wise man and it was *Draw-hondo-pico-say-nawk-limo* who asked, "Tell us the legend of the turkey."

"Yes," replied *Low-kay-dena-law-cheh-nenna*. "This is a legend indeed and I'm glad you were wise enough to inquire of it, for there is much to this story."

As *Low-kay-dena-law-cheh-neena* started his tale of the legend of the turkey, the young braves fell silent in interest to what they heard.

"The turkey was much like the peacock in the beginning. It could fly very long distances and was most beautiful to look upon. Its head was crowned with a magnificent headdress of red feathers and it could sing a thousand different tunes. The chief of the turkey was *Gaw-bel-lutak-pali-hanoo*.

One day, the Great Spirit, *Pawn-nay-leeki-taw-neh-nicco*, was glancing upon his creatures, when he saw *Gaw-bel-lutak-pali-hanoo* singing and flapping his beautiful wings before an audience of animals. It displeased *Pawn-nay-leeki-taw-neh-nicco* when he saw this, for he discovered that *Gaw-bel-lutak-pali-hanoo* did not sing praises in thanksgiving to him, but selfishly sang to receive the praise of others.

"This is not acceptable," said *Pawn-nay-leeki-taw-neh-nicco* to the many spirit braves who stood before his presence in his heavenly teepee. In unison, they all nodded in agreement.

The elder of the spirit braves asked, "And what shall be done to *Gaw-bel-lutak-pali-hanoo* for his insult to your goodness?"

"I will go down to him and counsel with him and see if he can be turned from his foolish path," said *Pawn-nay-leeki-taw-neh-nicco* in response to the question. All the spirit braves nodded in approval. The hosts of the heavenly teepee were glad to see the goodness of *Pawn-nay-leeki-taw-neh-nicco* displayed in mercy and not judgment; for that is what his name means: "Giver of Mercy and Not Judgment."

Descending to Earth, *Pawn-nay-leeki-taw-neh-nicco* transformed himself into a mangy dog. As he approached *Gaw-bel-lutak-pali-hanoo* to speak with him, *Gaw-bel-lutak-pali-hanoo* bolted upward and landed on a tree limb.

"What a disgusting looking creature you are," said *Gaw-bel-lutak-pali-hanoo.*

"What's wrong with me?" asked the dog.

"You look as though you need a bath and a good combing afterwards," laughed *Gaw-bel-lutak-pali-hanoo.*

"Looks aren't everything," snarled the dog in defense.

"Looks, my boy, are five-tenths of all that we are," continued *Gaw-bel-lutak-pali-hanoo.*

"Is that so?" asked the dog. "And what would be the other five-tenths?"

"Well, three-tenths goes to talent as you can clearly see that I have," said *Gaw-bel-lutak-pali-hanoo*, while following his statement with one of his wonderful songs that he knew.

"I can bark," said the dog and he barked a few times.

"Oh, please," said *Gaw-bel-lutak-pali-hanoo*, "you are an embarrassment to the rest of us creatures of the ancient land," he finished rudely.

"I see," said the dog, "so what comprises the final two-tenths you spoke of that I was lacking?"

"An audience," boomed *Gaw-bel-lutak-pali-hanoo.*

"I don't get it. What do you mean by having an audience?" questioned the dog once more.

"Must I spell it all out for you, you dumb dingo?" asked a condescending *Gaw-bel-lutak-pali-hanoo.*

"Yes, please explain it, for you have taught me much and you only need this little bit to finish the lesson you started with me," said the dog in a begging tone.

"Oh, very well," said *Gaw-bel-lutak-pali-hanoo.* "You don't have anyone who cares for you. No audience to feed you. No one to bathe you, to comb you, to praise you, and call out your name. No, you are a disgusting wild dog who has no one to care for you and that is the last two-tenths that you are missing."

Just then, the dog melted away and the Great Spirit, *Pawn-nay-leeki-taw-neh-nicco,* stepped forward to pass judgment on the arrogant turkey.

"You, *Gaw-bel-lutak-pali-hanoo,* represent the community of turkeys that exist within the ancient land and they have all followed your path of foolish pride. Because you condemned the dog and exalted yourself, I will change the status you so clearly spelled out. From now on, all turkeys will roam the ancient lands as wild creatures, while the dogs shall be domesticated and cared for by the *Mani-woo-ku-wok-kinosse* people. You will no longer be a free loader, but will have to search for your food and water. Because you condemned the dog for not having marvelous songs to sing, I will give him the howl that will be heard for miles in all directions, whereas instead of your thousands of songs, I will cause you and your descendants to only say your new name, *Gaw-bel,* for you are no longer worthy to wear the rest of your name. Because you boasted to the dog how pitiful he looked and how beautiful you were in comparison, I will melt the beautiful crown of red feathers and cause them to dangle down over your head and face, whereas the dog I will give many interesting coats of fur. But the worst of all these foolish things you practiced was the lack of thankfulness to me for blessing you with so many advantages over the other animals. For your refusal to give me thanksgiving, I will cause you to increase in size, where you will no longer be able to fly very far. You will be hunted and those that capture you will give me thanks for the grand feast that you will provide for them."

Then *Pawn-nay-leeki-taw-neh-nicco* walked upward into the clouds, leaving *Gaw-bel* to his fate.

When *Low-kay-dena-law-cheh-nenna* finished telling the legend of the turkey, he asked, "Now, my braves, does this story teach you something you can use?"

One-by-one, the braves got up, and as a brave would bow for permission to leave he would say, "Pride can only bring curses. I shall learn to praise others for their contributions." The wise man would smile and bow and the brave would exit.

Another brave bowed saying, "Life is not measured by how much we can take, but by how much we can offer back." Once again, the wise man smiled and bowed excusing his pupil.

As the last brave was leaving, *Low-kay-dena-law-cheh-nenna* realized that he did not offer up a comment on what he had learned.

"My son," *Low-kay-dena-law-cheh-nenna* asked, "did you not learn anything from the legend of the turkey?"

"Yes, master, I learned a great deal," replied the student.

"Why did you not give me your comment as the other braves did?" *Low-kay-dena-law-cheh-nenna* inquired further.

The young brave bowed and said, "I realized that in offering up my view on the lesson, it would be from the same pride that brought curses to *Gaw-bel*. I shall refrain from boasting about my newfound knowledge and shall submit my life to living out what I learn."

Low-kay-dena-law-cheh-nenna reached out to take the young brave by the hand as he said to him, "You have learned well, my son, and I choose you to be my replacement."

And with that said, the little brave grew strong in the knowledge of the *Mani-woo-ku-wok-kinosse* people and passed the knowledge down to where it is shared with you this day.

The Boy Who Did Not Fit In

Chapter One: Going to the Park

"It's a perfect day to go to the park and play," said Mr. Strong, as he shook his son, Robert, who was still lying in bed. "Get up, Robert," his dad commanded.

Robert jumped out of bed and made it because that is what he was taught to do when he awoke. Robert got cleaned, ate a hot breakfast, brushed his teeth, and got into the car with his dad. Robert and his dad arrived at the park and found that every child in town was there.

"Must I go, Dad?" inquired Robert.

"Yes, Robert, you do," stated Mr. Strong, "for how else can you make friends if you never meet them?"

"You know what, Robert?" questioned his dad. "Every friend was once a stranger." Mr. Strong continued his wise lecture by adding, "If all those children out there are strangers to you, then that means that every one of them could be your friend."

Robert's eyebrow rose as he thought of the prospect of having millions and billions of friends. Robert said, "I see your point, Dad," then ran off toward the playground.

When Robert got up to the other children, one of them said, "Hey, where did you get your clothes, at a garage sale?"

Another child said to Robert, "You are too little to play with us."

They asked him, "What's your name?" When Robert told them, they started calling him Robert the Robot. They began singing it over and over again, "Robert the Robot, Robert the Robot." Robert ran away and decided he would play without any of them. As he reached the slide, a large boy at the top said that he couldn't come up there because the slide belonged to him. Robert ran over to the merry-go-round, but the bigger kids had it going so fast that Robert was afraid to jump on it. Finally, he went over to the swings, but they were all taken. Robert decided that no one would be his friend and with tears in his eyes, he made his way back to his dad. Mr. Strong also had tears in his eyes because he felt so bad for his son. Mr. Strong thought to himself, *I was wrong for doing this to my little boy. When Robert gets to me, we will get into the car and go home and never come back to this wretched park.*

Chapter Three: The Pathway to Friendship

The more Robert thought of how awful his experience at the park was, the more he cried. Robert went over to the sandbox where a little girl his very age was playing.

The little girl asked him, "Why are you crying?"

Robert stopped and looked at her and said, "Because everybody here is mean."

"Am I mean?" asked the little girl.

Robert thought for a moment and then said, "No, I guess not."

"What is your name?" asked the little girl.

"My name is Robert. What is your name?" replied Robert to her.

"My name is Jessica; would you like to play with me?" Jessica said very politely.

Robert fell on his knees and grabbed a small plastic shovel and began to dig in the dirt. Mr. Strong sat back in his park bench wiping the tears that kept flowing from his eyes. Just moments before, Robert was running toward him crying and ready to quit and now he was playing with his new friend. All summer long, Robert and Jessica played together in the sandbox at the park. Before long, other parents saw what was going on and they would tell their children to go over to the sandbox and ask if they could also play, for they knew that Robert and Jessica would gladly say yes to them. Robert and Jessica stayed friends the rest of their lives and, when they got old enough, married each other.

Chapter Four: Twenty Years Later

"It's a perfect day to go to the park and play," said Robert as he shook his son, Jesse, who was still lying in bed. "Get up, Jesse," commanded his mother, Jessica.

Jesse jumped out of bed and made it because that is what he was taught to do when he awoke. Jesse got cleaned, ate a hot breakfast, brushed his teeth, and then got into the car with his mom and dad. As they headed toward the park, Robert and Jessica looked at each other thinking that today was the big day they had both been waiting for. When they arrived at the park, it seemed as though every kid in town was out there playing. Jesse didn't want to go into the park because he didn't know any of the kids. Robert told Jesse what his dad had told him about every friend was once a stranger. Before he headed off to make friends, his mother whispered something in his ear. As he was walking away, Robert turned to Jessica and asked her, "What was it you whispered in Jesse's ear?" Jessica said, "I told him that the sandbox was a good place to start looking for friends." Robert took Jessica into his arms and said, "Yes, my dear wife, the sandbox is a very good place to find friends."

The Girl Who Did Not Fit In

Chapter One: Going to the Park

"It's a perfect day to go to the park and play," said Mrs. Strong, as she shook her daughter, Rachael, who was still lying in bed. "Get up, Rachael," her mom commanded.

Rachael jumped out of bed and then made the bed, because that is what she was taught to do when she awoke. Rachael got cleaned, ate a hot breakfast, brushed her teeth, and then got into the car with her mom. Rachael and her mom arrived at the park and found that every child in town was there.

"Must I go, Mom?" inquired Rachael.

"Yes, Rachael, you do," stated Mrs. Strong, "for how else can you make friends if you never meet them?"

"You know what, Rachael?" questioned her mom. "Every friend was once a stranger." Mrs. Strong continued her wise lecture by adding, "If all those children out there are strangers to you, then that means that every one of them could be your friend."

Rachael's eyebrows rose as she thought of the prospect of having millions and billions of friends. Rachael said, "I see your point, Mom," and ran off toward the playground.

When Rachael got up to the other children, one of them said, "Hey, where did you get your clothes, at a garage sale?"

Another child said to Rachael, "You are too little to play with us."

They asked her, "What's your name?" When Rachael told them her name, the children started calling her Rachael the Robot. They began singing it over and over again, "Rachael the Robot, Rachael the Robot."

Rachael ran away and decided she would play without any of them. As Rachael reached the slide, a large girl at the top said that she could not come up there, because the slide belonged to her. Rachael ran over to the merry-go-round, but the bigger kids had it going so fast that Rachael was afraid to jump on it. Finally, she went over to the swings, but they were all taken. Rachael decided that no one would be her friend and, with tears in her eyes, she made her way back to her mom.

Mrs. Strong also had tears in her eyes because she felt so bad for her daughter, Rachael. Mrs. Strong thought to herself, *I was wrong for doing this to my little girl. When Rachael gets to me, we will get into the car and go home and never come back to this wretched park.*

Chapter Three: The Pathway to Friendship

The more Rachael thought of how awful her experience at the park was, the more she cried. Rachael was walking through the sandbox where a little boy her very age was playing.

The little boy asked her, "Why are you crying?"

Rachael stopped and looked at him and said, "Because everybody here is mean."

"Am I mean?" asked the little boy.

Rachael thought for a moment and said, "No, I guess not."

"What is your name?" the little boy asked.

"My name is Rachael; what is your name?" asked Rachael.

"My name is Jonathon; would you like to play with me?" Jonathon said very politely.

Rachael fell on her knees and grabbed a small plastic shovel and began to dig in the dirt. Mrs. Strong sat back in her park bench wiping the tears that kept flowing from her eyes. Just moments before, Rachael was running toward her crying and ready to quit and now she was playing with her new friend.

All summer long, Rachael and Jonathon played together in the sandbox at the park. Before long, other parents saw what was going on and they would tell their children to go over to the sandbox and ask if they could also play, for they knew that Rachael and Jonathon would gladly say yes to them. Rachael and Jonathon stayed friends the rest of their lives and, when they got old enough, married each other.

"It's a perfect day to go to the park and play," said Rachael as she shook her son, Johnny, who was still lying in bed. "Get up, Johnny," commanded his dad, Jonathon.

Johnny jumped out of bed and then made the bed, because that is what he was taught to do when he awoke. Johnny got cleaned, ate a hot breakfast, brushed his teeth, and then got into the car with his mom and dad. As they headed toward the park, Rachael and Jonathon looked at each other thinking that today was the big day they had both been waiting for. When they arrived at the park, it seemed as though every kid in town was out there playing. Johnny didn't want to go into the park because he didn't know any of the kids. Rachael told Johnny what her mom told her about every friend was once a stranger. Before he headed off to make friends, his dad whispered something in his ear.

As Johnny walked away, Rachael turned to Jonathon and asked him, "What was it you whispered in Johnny's ear?"

Jonathon said, "I told him that the sandbox was a good place to start looking for friends."

Rachael took Jonathon into her arms and said, "Yes, my dear husband, the sandbox is a very good place to find friends."

The Sick Troll

Chapter One: Coming Down With Something

Bramble was a disgusting troll who lived in the dark places of the earth. He favored dwelling within holes located underneath tree roots that overhung dried out riverbeds or beneath bridges. These places stayed cool, were not in the direct path of the sun, and they were places that unsuspecting travelers would eventually pass by so he could harass them for food and possessions. Because sunlight will burn any troll's hide, they only move around outside after the sun has gone down and return to their dens before the morning sunrise.

The people of Western Forest gave Bramble his name, for he was a thorn to them in how he threatened the good people with severe beatings if they did not share their goods with him. The wise king tried in vain to capture Bramble so he could imprison him for his crimes, but the sheriffs were always unable to find him. The time came when the king became preoccupied with greater affairs and thus forgot all about Bramble and his delinquent behavior.

Late one evening, a drunken traveler came to the bridge that Bramble lived under. The man was Cicero, a local tavern owner. Cicero, not feeling well for several days, went to the capitol city to have himself checked by the doctor. Thus, returning with medicine to take before he goes to bed, Cicero took advantage of the long walk home by consuming a good amount of wine.

"Halt," said Bramble the troll. "Who dares cross my bridge at night, without invitation or permission?"

"It is Cic — Cic — Cicero," said Cicero with some difficulty.

"Cicero," laughed Bramble. "Shouldn't it be Sissy Rose?"

"Hold your tongue, sir, and remove yourself from my path or I will be forced to bean you with my cane," said Cicero as he swung the cane, and then staggered somewhat from losing his balance.

Bramble laughed as he said, "You drunken old codger, you couldn't hit the wind during a tornado if you tried. Now, unload what is left of your wine and victuals that you are carrying back with you and I will let you pass over my bridge without giving you a severe beating."

"You mistake me, Sir Troll, for one who scares easily from things that are both ugly and smell badly," said Cicero in a tone of utter disgust. "But because I need to get home, you may keep what remains of my goods, so that I may make haste to my bed."

Then, without any further ado, Cicero dropped his pack that contained both food and drink and staggered past Bramble with no further incident.

Bramble picked up the bag, slightly irritated that he had been deprived of the chance to beat the tavern owner and then take his bag by force. Regardless of the ease at which he obtained his meal, Bramble scurried off to his hole and set out to feast upon what Cicero gave him. Ironically, though Cicero had been robbed of his food, he was able to get the last laugh between Bramble and himself because he was able to give Bramble the illness that was afflicting him. Little about illnesses was known in those days and when Bramble's lips touched the wine bottle that Cicero had been drinking from, he immediately fell ill himself. Though there is no recorded disease that is lethal to trolls, many of them still cause trolls to feel badly and Bramble realized that he was coming down with something.

Chapter Two: Eavesdropping

After three days, Bramble finally regained enough strength to crawl out of his hole and get some fresh, night air. He sat against one of the legs that supported the bridge and there, tried to clear his head of the cobwebs that seemed to clutter his thoughts. With each deep breath, Bramble felt a little better.

It was at midnight that Bramble heard the sounds of approaching horsemen. He could make out some clanging sounds that are made by metal.

"Knights," Bramble said to himself. "I am in no condition to fight a knight and two knights would surely defeat me with ease. I will have to let them pass and hope they do so without noticing me." Bramble lay quietly on the ground as he stared up at the deck of the bridge.

Upon approaching the bridge, the horsemen dismounted and walked their steeds cautiously across. They did so because of the fear that a horse could possibly break through the deck and sustain a serious injury to its leg. It was at the halfway point of the bridge that the knights halted and began to talk of secret things. It was not Bramble's intention to listen in on the pointless jabbering of men, but due to his present situation, he found himself eavesdropping onto their conversation.

Knight Michaelson spoke first by asking, "Will your men be ready to storm the castle by the end of spring?"

"Yes, my Lord," said knight Blackshore. "All that remains for us to do is begin the distraction that will cause the king to dispatch his forces away from the castle. Once the cavalry has been drawn away to squelch the uprising, a few of our loyalists on the inside will let the drawbridge down. Our army will enter the castle and capture the king. Then you, Lord Michaelson, will assume your rightful place upon the throne and King Edward's name will be remembered no more."

Bramble shook in anger as he listened to what the knights were saying amongst themselves. Though Bramble was a troubling thief to all who crossed his bridge, he was still a patriotic citizen toward his homeland and desperately disliked anyone who would betray their king. "It should never be heard in any kingdom," said Bramble to himself, "that a knight should harm his king. I must do what I can to stop knights Michaelson and Blackshore, before they succeed in their evil plans."

Chapter Three: Fugitive Apprehended

As the day began to break, Bramble hid himself inside his hole and rested until he could come out again. At the setting of the sun, Bramble left his home and set out toward the castle. Unsure of how he could gain access to the king, Bramble walked with a noble purpose at heart in hopes of saving his king.

At the drawbridge, the Keep cried out, "Who goes there?"

"It is I, Bramble the troll, and I have come to fight your strongest man in a duel," said Bramble arrogantly.

Quickly a runner was dispatched to find the commander of the watch. When the commander heard of the troll's appearance, he was surprised to find him so handy for capture. The drawbridge lowered and Commander Pyke stepped forward.

"I am Commander Pyke of the king's security forces," said Commander Pyke. "I warn you, troll Bramble not to attempt escape, for I have archers on the wall who will not miss on their first release," Pyke warned sternly.

Bramble knew that this was the only way to get close to the king, so he said, "Don't shoot me and I will not resist arrest."

Bramble was arrested and taken to the lower dungeon and kept there until word arrived from the king as to what should be done with him.

The next morning, as the king was being fed his breakfast, Commander Pyke arrived at his door and waited for his invitation to see the king.

An aide came to the door and said, "His majesty has heard that you bring good news and has asked for your presence."

As the commander stepped into the dining hall, the herald announced, "Commander Pyke at your service, my Lord."

"Ah, Commander Pyke," the king said with enthusiasm in his voice. "Please come closer and share with me your report."

"My Lord," Commander Pyke said with a respectful bow, "I have good news that you have waited to hear for some time now. A fugitive has been apprehended who has been at-large for many years and is being held in the lower dungeon."

With a giant smile on his face, the king asked knowingly, "Bramble?"

"Yes, my Lord, Bramble is now in custody and we await your decision on what shall be done to him," the commander replied.

The king pondered what would be done with Bramble as he crunched into another slice of bacon. "Commander," inquired the king with keen suspicion, "tell me, how were you able to apprehend Bramble last night, when all the sheriffs in my kingdom have failed to accomplish this in over twenty-four years?"

"Ah, um, well that is the oddity of it all, my Lord," the commander stuttered.

"Oddity?" repeated the king, "In what way?"

"Bramble approached the castle wall last night and challenged the strongest man to come out and fight him," Commander Pyke said reluctantly.

"Indeed, that is odd," said the king. "I would like very much to interview Bramble personally. Cause him to have his arms chained to the walls to ensure my safety and then I will talk privately with him," the king ordered with a piercing glance at the commander.

The commander snapped his heels and said quickly, "It shall be done with haste, my Lord," and with a proper bow, the commander left with a purpose in his stride.

A room was cleared and made ready for the king's use in interrogating Bramble. With a hood over his head, Bramble trusted in his heart that no matter what may befall him, he at least tried to save his king. Upon entering a well-lit room, heavy chains were shackled onto Bramble's legs and arms. Bramble knew what this meant and when the hood was taken off his head, the guards were surprised to find a troll with an ear-to-ear smile on his face.

Upon the arrival of the king, the guards left the area, for they knew better than to pry into the affairs of state.

Bramble bowed his head upon the entrance of the king. At seeing this, the king was growing surer of his suspicions that Bramble purposefully staged his own arrest.

"Tell me something, Bramble," the king began his conversation, "how is it that my most wanted fugitive for over twenty-four years all of a sudden shows up at my front door and announces his presence? Tell me something else, while you are at it; how is it that a thief and a crude thug such as you bows when he sees me in person, but shows no respect to my laws or any other person in my kingdom?"

Bramble bowed again and said in a humble manner, "Most assuredly, the king is right in his suspicions, and nothing is hidden from his thought-filled glance. What I have done cannot be explained apart from an emergency of such grand magnitude that it propels me toward this self-destructive course of action. Oh, King Edward, upon the third night beforehand, I lay under the bridge at Bailey's Bend and overheard two of your highest lords plotting against you. It is for no other reason that I have made myself an easy capture, in order that I may save your life. By the expense of my own life, I have caused our meeting to occur in order that I may warn you of a coming disaster."

After the king heard what Bramble said, he instructed the guards not to harm the troll. The king also ordered them to make sure that Bramble was fed the officer's portion every day until he was brought before the court to stand trial. Commander Pyke was pleased to hear that the king made mention of Bramble's trial and no one had the slightest idea of all that the king learned during his private investigation.

Chapter Four: Spring Cleaning

In the next county, a riot broke out in the town of Clarkshire. The few sheriffs that were responsible for that area were unable to regain control and a dispatch was sent to inform the king of the desperate situation. Like clockwork, the king ordered his cavalry to speedily descend upon Clarkshire and re-establish the peace. Within minutes, the cavalry was racing down the highway and the king sat at his throne and carried on as though nothing happened.

Just as the hourglass was ready to be turned, a trumpet from outside the walls of the castle was heard. There, marching down the highway was a band of about one thousand men. Knight Michaelson led the forward group of five hundred strong and Blackshore led the rear group of five hundred more. As the king looked out from his battlement, he could see his two knights approaching with full confidence in their victory.

The drawbridge lowered to meet the advancing army and Michaelson and his five hundred entered as the drawbridge closed behind them. From behind Blackshore's formation, the king's cavalry filtered out of the tree line and began their attack. Blackshore and his column were taken completely by surprise and they met their just rewards there on the eastern lawn of Castle Edward.

Michaelson turned to see the castle drawbridge close behind him. A shout came from the wall as Commander Pyke order a volley of arrows. The battle was quick and the traitors saw the fruit of their labor in the wrath of their king's great displeasure. You can read of the defeat of Michaelson and Blackshore in the annals of King Edward.

Chapter Five: "How Do You Plead?"

The day for Bramble's trial came and the king sat on his throne with royal pomp. It was ordered that the troll be bathed and dressed with a suitable set of clothes so such a disheveled creature would not embarrass the court.

Bramble was brought before the king and once again to the surprise of the king and all his subjects, the troll bowed in true admiration and respect.

The court opened with the clerk describing Bramble, what crimes he was being charged with, and the parties that sought their claims of restitution. Then the king asked, "Bramble, you are accused of these many crimes? The court wishes to know: how do you plead?"

Bramble bowed once again to his king and said, "I plead guilty to all charges laid before me this day."

The king was somewhat puzzled at Bramble's bold plea and inquired, "Bramble, do you know what you have just said and the consequences that such words hold for you?"

Bramble once again bowed and said, "Yes, my Lord, King Edward, I do know what it is I am doing to myself. Had I pleaded innocent, I would have been entitled to a fair trial, but because I have pleaded guilty, I can place myself before the mercy of the court and beg the court's forgiveness for my many evil deeds."

The king was tremendously pleased to hear this response and he congratulated the troll on his wise actions and words. The king went on to remind the audience that it was Bramble who put his own life in danger in order to save the life of his king.

"In my entire kingdom," King Edward preached, "I have never met anyone who was so willing to protect me. Only my knights have proven such valor and devotion. How wrong it would be to harm such a one who possesses such devotion as he does for his king. Bramble not only saved my life, but the lives of us all. Our kingdom is safe today because Bramble loved his king so much that he was willing to lay down his life for my well-being. Let the goodness of Bramble return upon his own head as I pass this verdict: Bramble, because you were willing to humbly admit your many crimes instead of lying to the court by falsely pleading innocent, I declare you justified of your many offenses. I extend to you a full pardon and I proudly give to you a full restoration of rights as a citizen of this kingdom."

Before Bramble could respond, the king continued by saying, "My castle has a big drawbridge in front of it, but it doesn't have a drawbridge guard who would faithfully keep it safe at night. Bramble, would you do the king's service by moving from the bridge at Bailey's Bend to my drawbridge?"

Bramble was deeply touched by the mercy and goodness of his king and he humbly accepted the king's pardon and invitation to serve as the drawbridge guard. It is said that Bramble never beat anyone up for food after that, for the kind citizens of King Edward's kingdom gladly brought him food. Not only did he have the food from the local people, but the king ordered a daily ration to be brought to him exactly at sundown.

Many years have passed since Bramble lived under the king's drawbridge, but legend says that his soul lingers on in objects that were made by human hands like bridges and castle walls. The powerful love of Bramble survives in order to protect the interest of his king. So it is that if ever you find yourself whispering secrets to one another, remember this saying well: *The walls have ears and every secret shared is a secret no longer.*

The Stingy Farmer

Chapter One: The New Law

King Waldon was a fair and wise king who ruled his people well. One day, the books were opened for review where the king noticed that large revenues were being spent on feeding the castle staff and the security forces that stayed there in order to keep the king safe.

"The cost of feeding the staff and security forces is deplorable," said the king with a concerned voice. He continued by asking, "What is the percentage taken from the gross of our tax base in order to feed the staff?"

"My Lord," said the bookkeeper, "It appears that 28 percent of all your yearly income goes to this one expenditure."

King Waldon snapped his fingers and an aide appeared and said, "My Lord?"

The king said, "Assemble my advisory counsel in the great chamber so we can discuss our options on how to remedy my budget."

"Yes, my Lord," the aide replied and then left in haste to gather the counselors for the meeting.

At the budget meeting, the king told his counselors of his great dislike of having to spend huge portions of the nation's taxes just to feed his staff. After hearing the king's concerns, the advisers huddled together and discussed the situation among themselves.

"My Lord," the chief adviser petitioned, "we, the counsel, have come to a determination that we believe will work extremely well."

"Say on," the king commanded.

The chief adviser continued, "It is believed that the king is paying for something that actually belongs to him in the first place. Because the king owns all lands, it is true, then, that all things either grown from the land or raised upon the land are a byproduct of the king's goodness. We advise you, sire, to enact a new law that would require every farmer in your kingdom to provide your Chief Cook with enough food to feed all of the king's staff and security forces for one entire day. Every farmer would do this just one time every year without charging the bookkeeper, for it will be offered as a gift of both patriotism and gratitude to their king. Each farmer will be issued a date and on that date they must bring their gifts of food. Anyone unwilling to bring the king their gift will be considered unpatriotic and ungrateful to their king and the staff that serves him, and that person will be subject to severe penalties for such treason."

King Waldon leaned back on his throne as he said to the counsel, "What you say is extremely wise and good for the kingdom. I therefore decree that starting on the first of the new year, the Gift Law shall begin. Anyone not willing to bring their king a gift of food to feed his staff for a day, will be breaking the law and subject to severe penalties."

Nelson was a highly successful farmer and, when he heard of the new law, he was pleased that he could do his part to support his king. As he was outside planting one of his fields, one of the king's aides rode up with a scribe and asked him his name.

"My name is Nelson of Barlow County," Nelson said to the king's aide as he gave a bow of respect.

The aide turned to the scribe and said, "Nelson, two-forty-eight."

The scribe wrote the name and number down and then looked on his calendar for the date.

"The date of your food gift to the king will be on September the eleventh," the aide instructed. Nelson bowed as he said, "It would be my pleasure to bring my gift to our great king."

With that said, the king's aides rode off to the next farm.

One day, Nelson was visiting the walled city where the castle was, in order to deliver the goods he brought to the differing businesses that used his products. There were so many things that he brought that it took the best part of the day to make all the deliveries. Due to the night closing in on him, he decided to stay at the inn and head back home when morning came. His room was on the second floor and it had a view of the main street below.

The next morning, Nelson was up bright and early preparing his cart for departure. As he was harnessing his ox to the cart, he heard horses trotting down the main road in his direction. As he turned, he was shocked to find that the king was out riding through town with an armed escort. When the king came near, Nelson bowed low to show his respect. Once the company of riders was past him, Nelson rose up from his bow and viewed the king as he rode on.

"My goodness," Nelson said to himself. "The king is getting very fat. If he doesn't take better care of himself, we will be out of a good king and it is unlikely we will ever have another king that is both wise and kind."

Just as Nelson was lamenting over the king's obesity, a farmer with a cart loaded down with food slowly made his way past him.

"Where are you going?" Nelson inquired.

"I am Thoran of Contulmire County, and I have the good

pleasure of bringing the king my food gift today," the passing farming explained.

Nelson, curious as to what the king was eating that was making him so fat and unhealthy, asked farmer Thoran, "May I see what you bring the king's staff, so I may know what I should bring when it is my day?"

"Please do," farmer Thoran said as he lifted the sheet that covered the food he had in his cart.

"I notice that you bring the king the very best of delicacies," Nelson said, complimenting the farmer.

"Yes," said Thoran. "The king will be pleased with my gift, for I bring the richest pastries and meat that still has lots of fat left on it, so it will have greater flavor. I also bring candies and snacks that the king may enjoy throughout the day."

"I see," said Nelson. "So you are bringing food that you think will catch the king's attention and are hoping that after he has eaten your gift, he will want to meet and honor you for such wonderful treats."

The conversation had Nelson concerned for his king, for he knew that everyone who brought food did so to impress the king and did not consider how they were harming him with their food gifts.

"It seems to me," Nelson said to himself, "that the good people of our kingdom are loving our dear king to death. I shall have to consider well what gift I bring him when September the eleventh arrives."

Chapter Three: The Stingy Farmer

Nelson traveled throughout the night in order to arrive at the castle early enough to deliver his food gift before breakfast began. The Chief Cook and his staff unloaded Nelson's cart and Nelson took the time to explain to the cook how his gift was to be given then he departed for home.

The cook was reluctant to feed the king what Nelson brought, but there was no other food available to prepare. As the server lifted the dome covering the platter, the king's mouth fell open.

"Bring me the cook," the king ordered.

The cook bowed and said, "My Lord?"

"What is the meaning of serving me oatmeal for breakfast?" the king boomed in disgust.

"My Lord, this is the gift that the farmer brought you and your staff," the cook said apologetically.

"This is preposterous," the king said, enraged as he shoved the bowl away from him. "You very well know that I always eat eggs, bacon, sausage, and pancakes covered in lots of butter and syrup," he continued sputtering.

"Yes, my Lord, I know your menu well, but I can only cook what is brought to me by your farmers," the cook replied back.

"Indeed, so what did the farmer bring me for lunch and dinner?" inquired the king in order to make himself feel better about missing breakfast.

"My Lord," the cook said as sweat began running down his brow, "the farmer brought you beans and cornbread for lunch and a simple salad with no dressing for dinner."

The king rose in great wrath and called for the captain of the guard. Before the captain could make his way halfway down the dining hall, the king called out to him and ordered, "Bring back to me the stingy farmer who dared to insult me and my staff with this lousy food gift."

"Yes, my Lord," the captain said as he slid on his feet to stop and reverse his direction. A detachment of riders rushed out of the walled city and headed down the road that led in the direction of Barlow County.

Chapter Four: This Better Be Good

Nelson was arrested and brought back to the castle in a caged wagon. As the wagon made its way through the streets of the walled city, the people who lived there came out in order to taunt him for bringing the king a bad food gift. "Here's a gift for you, Nelson," one of the townspeople said as he threw a rotten tomato at him. When other bystanders saw this, they also made insults and threw things at Nelson.

When the caged wagon arrived at the castle, the guards took Nelson to the great chamber and placed him in the middle of the room. Against the walls were seated all of the king's advisers who conjured up the Gift Law, the king's staff, and a small number of lawyers.

The crier announced the king, and all the assembly rose as the king entered the great chamber. As the king sat, the assembly also sat.

Ardon, who is the king's personal lawyer, began the proceeding with his opening statement. "At the first of the year, King Waldon enacted a new law whereby all farmers of the kingdom were to bring the king and his staff, food for an entire day, one day a year. So far, we have had great success in this practice except for one stingy farmer who decided he would bring such a pitiful gift as to mock our good king and his staff. The assembly demands that farmer Nelson explain to those present why he brought such a gift this morning."

As Ardon lowered himself down onto his chair, he popped back up and said with a humorous tone in his voice, "And, Nelson, this better be good."

The great chamber echoed from the laughter that filled it. The king and his noble lords could not stop themselves from laughing any longer. None of them could believe that there was someone in their kingdom who was so crass as to do the foolish thing that Nelson had done.

Nelson stood before them with food slime still running down his clothes. With proper etiquette, Nelson bowed to the king, and then to each group assembled.

"My Lord, King Waldon, and noble staff," Nelson began his

defense, "I know that what I did today has confused you all and that my gift seemed quite offensive when compared to what others had already given in days before, but I assure you that I would never do anything to insult my king or his noble lords, for they have been faithful ministers of our welfare for many years now. I especially am devoted to you and your will. Months ago, I was staying at the Main Street Inn when, upon the morning of my departure, the king with his escort came riding through town. As the company rode past me, I arose from my bow, in order to see my king before he was out of view. What I saw disturbed me, for my king had gained much weight from just six months earlier. After seeing what the others were bringing him to eat, I determined in my heart that I would not feed the king such foods as to obtain his praise at the expense of his health. I decided that I would feed him not more, not sweeter, not tastier foods, but foods that were healthy, for I want my king to live a long time. Ask yourselves if your own mothers would feed you food that she knew would weaken your body and make you unhealthy. Therefore, my conscience will only allow me to do what is right for my king, in spite of how unpopular or inconvenient it is to me. With that said, I rest my case and return the remainder of my time back to the court for its judgment."

The lords were silent, for they knew that the farmer was right in his actions. They also knew that they had often played up to the king instead of acting in his best interest. As Ardon attempted to rise out of his seat, the king snapped at him and said, "Stay seated, man, for your services are no longer needed."

"Well, farmer Nelson," the king said. "It seems that we all mistook your intentions. I didn't consider the reason behind your gift, because I was too preoccupied focusing on the kind of gift you brought to me. I was thinking of myself; whereas, you were thinking about my health. Who in my entire kingdom is this honest with their king? While everyone is attempting to impress me, you are trying to improve me. Your actions have inspired me, farmer Nelson, and that is why I decree that all food gifts must be prepared with the health of the king and his staff in mind. I also wish to extend to farmer Nelson my invitation to join my advisory committee."

Thus, Nelson became one of the king's advisers because he was willing to do what was right instead of what was popular. The king and his lords lived long and healthy lives and many people practiced Nelson's wise eating habits, causing the entire kingdom to prosper.

Trailer Trash

Chapter One: How to Have a Bad Day

"Molly," inquired Mrs. Praxton of her daughter.

"What?" Molly answered back with an unhappy voice.

"Well," her mother continued, "how was your first day at school?"

Molly plopped herself on the couch and curled her knees up to her chest and said blankly, "It was the most horrible time I've ever had at any school."

Mrs. Praxton picked Molly's head up as she scooted her lap underneath her. Mrs. Praxton ran her fingers through Molly's long beautiful hair as she asked, "Will you tell me what happened at school today or must I call your teacher to find out?"

There was a short silence and then Molly said, "Mother, we were all out in the playground having fun, when some of the kids walked up to me and began teasing me."

"Now, Molly, they don't even know you yet; what could they possibly have to say to you?" questioned her mother further.

Raising her voice some, Molly said, "They started saying that because we live in a mobile home at Sunny Meadows Trailer Park, that I was trailer trash. They just kept saying it over and over again. I didn't know what to say back. They even snickered at me on the bus and when I got off, Billy Crittenton said, 'See you later, trailer trash.'"

"Oh, my," said Mrs. Praxton. "This is serious. I'm glad you told me what was going on."

"What are you going to do about it, Mom," Molly asked with a hopeful look on her face.

"Now don't you worry about that, young lady," said Mrs. Praxton with a smile on her face, "Your ol' mom knows how to fix just about everything."

Molly was glad that she shared her problem with her mom and they both hugged. Then Molly raced out to the back yard to play with her dogs.

While Molly was outside, Mrs. Praxton called Molly's teacher, Miss Singleton, and Mrs. Howton, the principal, to discuss Molly's problem with them.

Chapter Two: The Assignment

The following day, the school bell rang and all of the children dashed to stand in line in front of their teachers. As the teachers began counting their students, Miss Singleton noticed that Molly was at the end of the line. This bothered Miss Singleton to see this, for she remembered being treated this very same way when she was in school. As the students sat at their desks, Miss Singleton called the roll.

"Okay, class," Miss Singleton continued, "there is a special project I want you to have ready by tomorrow. Because we know so little of each other, I want us to have a show-and-tell day. Miss Singleton began drawing a stick person on the chalkboard and then she placed a question mark in the middle of its round head.

Miss Singleton explained further by saying, "I feel that we know very little about each other and I thought it would be appropriate to change this. Tomorrow will be our first show-and-tell day and each student is required to bring something. They will show the object and then tell us what the object means to you. It can be a craft, a collection, or anything that best describes what you like, who you are, or what you like to do."

All the children made noises of their excitement and approval. When class was finished for the day, they ran out to their buses, impatient to get home and start putting together their items that they would bring back with them to school the next day.

On the bus, Billy Crittenton couldn't wait for Molly to walk past him as she was leaving. "See you later, trailer trash," Billy said with a smirk on his face. Molly walked past him and acted as though she didn't hear him.

Chapter Three: Finding It

"Mom, I'm home," Molly shouted as she dashed to her room.

Mrs. Praxton walked into Molly's room, finding Molly busy picking through her closet.

"What are you looking for, Molly?" asked Mrs. Praxton with a giant smile on her face.

"Something to take to school tomorrow for show-and-tell," Molly said as she continued working like a badger who was busy digging a hole in the ground.

"Show-and-tell," squeaked Mrs. Praxton. "Oh, I used to love those days," she continued her jubilant recollection.

"We have to bring something that we are currently doing or something that we like more than anything in the world," Molly instructed her mom further.

"Well, stop a minute and let us see if we can think about what it is you like the most, before you manage to throw everything you own out on the floor," said Mrs. Praxton as she sat on Molly's bed.

Molly backed out of her closet and sat next to her mom. They intently thought about finding it as they looked around the room. A picture of her dad hung on the wall. Molly leaned against her mom and said in a hushed voice, "I sure miss Daddy."

"I miss him, too," said Mrs. Praxton as she leaned her head against Molly's.

"You know, Molly," continued her mom, "you could take dad's picture to school and tell everybody about him, if you want."

"Oh, Mom, could I really?" Molly asked with her eyes glistening.

"Sure you can," Mrs. Praxton said back. "And I have a secret to share with you," she continued saying.

"What is it, Mom?" Molly asked excitedly.

Mrs. Praxton put her hands on both sides of her mouth and whispered in Molly's ear, "Your teacher and the principal have combined their efforts and are going to bring their own show-and-tell to share with all of the class tomorrow."

"Wow," said Molly. "I can't begin to imagine what that could be."

"Well, I can't either," said Mrs. Praxton, as she jumped to her feet, "But if you have found your show-and-tell object, then I say we need to go to the kitchen and make us some oatmeal raisin cookies and then pig out on them."

"I get to do the stirring," said Molly as they scrambled to the kitchen to have some fun.

Chapter Four: Show Day

It was show-and-tell day and the children had the same excited energy as if they were at a carnival. Miss Singleton calmed the class down and then called for Billy Crittenton to show first. Billy pulled out a baseball that had a bunch of signatures on it and a box that had hundreds of baseball cards in it. He told of the game where his dad caught the ball he brought and how they got to go down and meet the players and get them to sign it. He said he liked nothing more than going to the ballpark with his dad and watching his favorite team play.

One-by-one, the children showed their items. There were video games, collections of bugs, and dolls. Some of the children brought awards and others played instruments.

They all got to show their items and then the teacher said, "I've been noticing that Molly is always the last one in line, so I decided to let her go last since this is the way she is treated around here." The classroom went from noisy to a stilled quiet. The children weren't expecting to hear something like that and they definitely weren't ready for what Molly had to say either.

Molly walked to the front of the classroom holding the picture of her dad. She held it in front of her as she said, "This is my dad. Everybody called him Mac, but his real name is John. I would have brought him today, instead of this picture, but I couldn't because he isn't living anymore. My daddy was killed in a combat mission as he and his fellow soldiers were fighting terrorists. My mom tells me that many people are free there now and that children just like us get to go to school for the first time in their lives. I miss my daddy all the time and I wish I could go with him to just one ball game. I'd like to play a video game with him. My dolls sit on their shelves waiting for him to walk through the door so we can play house, but he never comes."

As Molly talked, her mom walked into the classroom and sat down at the front of the class. Molly ran over to her and sat in her lap as she finished saying, "This is my mom and she is my best friend."

Billy Crittenton's heart nearly exploded when he realized just how much Molly had already suffered from losing her dad. His eyes began to tear up as he sat frozen in his chair.

Just then, the principal walked through the door and announced that there would be an assembly inside the auditorium in fifteen minutes.

Chapter Five: The Assembly

Once Miss Singleton's class had been seated on the front row, an announcement was made over the loudspeakers informing all the classes that there was a special, unscheduled assembly being held in the auditorium and that all students were required to attend.

On the stage was a row of chairs that stretched across its length. There was a podium in front of them that was equipped with a microphone.

The principal walked behind the podium and started the special event by stating, "Dear guests, it is my great pleasure to have outstanding members of our community visit our school today. These men and women are those who helped pioneer our town and help shape it into the wonderful place we call home, today. Please offer them a warm welcome." Then Mrs. Howton turned toward the direction of the curtains and began to applaud. One-by-one, adults began walking onto the stage.

As the applause died down, Mrs. Howton said, "Mrs. Penny Hamilton, please come forward and start our community history conference."

Mrs. Hamilton was very old and using her walker, she worked her way to the podium. She had a big smile on her face and was pleased she could speak to the children that day.

"My dear children," she said as though they really were her own kids. "Many of you I held in my arms when you were first born for I was the nurse who helped deliver you. I am retired now and don't do much. I can't mow my own lawn anymore and I don't need a large place to live so I live in a mobile home at the Sunny Meadows Trailer Park. They keep the grass mowed and someone is always dropping in on me to see how I'm doing." When she mentioned where she lived, many of the children turned and looked at each other.

John Angleton came forward next and told the children, "I was a truck driver for over thirty-five years. I eventually had to stop driving because my back got ruined from driving for long periods every day. Although my back hurts all the time now, I'm glad I was able to do my part to make life easier for everybody else. If any of you kids are ever in my neighborhood, be sure to wave. I live over at

Sunny Meadows Trailer Park and am generally sitting outside on the porch in my rocking chair."

Once again, the children turned and looked at each other when they learned where Mr. Angleton lived.

Lonnie Johnston shared his story of working in the oil fields and how dangerous the work was. He had fun showing them that two fingers were missing from his left hand.

Jamie Carlton recalled her years as a school teacher and how she had to stop when she was diagnosed with cancer. She was almost through with her chemotherapy and couldn't wait to get back to teaching.

Marion Morton still runs the movie theater downtown. She says that she always puts lots of butter on the popcorn.

Damion Thorton used to be a fireman, but the smoke eventually hurt his lungs, which forced him to quit. Now he's a mechanic for the city.

Georgette Washington cuts and styles hair at the beauty salon. She claims to know everybody in town or at least somebody who knows those she doesn't know.

Tom Willington is still the editor at the newspaper and he coaches the swim team at the YMCA.

Jennifer Clayton is the librarian and is the president of the Geese Lodge.

Dirk Houston is a retired electrician who spends his time taking pictures at weddings.

Amazingly, all of the guests present had one thing in common with each other: they all lived at Sunny Meadows Trailer Park.

When the guests were done speaking, the principal stepped forward and said, "Today, I saw and heard from a group of wonderful people. One was a librarian and another one is a coach. I heard from a newspaper editor, a beautician, a fireman, a mechanic, a business owner, a cancer survivor, a teacher, a truck driver, and a nurse. Ask yourself, who was it that you heard from today?"

Just then, Billy Crittenton jumped up and shouted, "Trailer treasure!" over and over again. Soon all the children were helping Billy say it. Molly and her mother hugged each other as they realized that *One bully's trash is another school's treasure.* Ironically, Billy Crittenton became Molly's best friend at school and he looked after her as though she were his little sister.

As the bell rang that very next day, Miss Singleton went to the front door of the school to let the children come inside. When she opened the door, she was pleased to see that Molly was the first person standing in line.

Two Little Love Birds

Chapter One: An Open Window Invitation

As the sun began to come into view, two little love birds were sitting on a branch, one was Drake and the other one was Daisy. They began their day singing about those things that they liked doing or about those whom they loved.

"I love you, Drake," Daisy sang.

"And I love you, Daisy," said Drake singing back.

"I really like to fly up high and fast," Daisy finished her lyrics.

"Oh, me too," Drake confessed then continued his solo by saying, "and I really like to hug and snuggle when we land on a branch." With that being said, the two little love birds embraced each other with a warm, feathery hug.

As they sat on the branch hugging and chirping, they both noticed an open window at the house below them.

Daisy asked, "Are you thinking what I'm thinking?"

"Yes, my fair feathered friend," Drake gladly responded. "We should go and investigate."

"Humans are very smart land dwellers who can build anything they want," Daisy said with a tone of enthusiasm.

"Indeed, there is nothing smarter than a human and we could learn much about love if we took the time to watch them," Drake said in agreement back.

So the two little love birds decided to watch people in order to learn more about love.

Chapter Two: Bigger Isn't Always Better

"It's mine," squealed one child to the other.

"No, it isn't. I had it first," replied the other child who pulled the doll out of the other one's hand.

"Oh, my," said Daisy. "These children are not sharing their toys with each other."

Drake agreed and said, "This is true, for they are not only fighting, but they are refusing to practice love, which gladly gives to those it loves. The doll they fought over has a broken leg and its hair is beyond combing."

Drake and Daisy flew away and found themselves at another open window nearby and so they landed on its sill and began listening to the person inside.

A woman was on the phone crying, "I'll never forgive you for what you did to me. I hope you suffer as you have made me suffer."

A voice from the phone said back, "I'm truly sorry for what I did to you. Please don't stay mad at me any longer, but forgive me, so that we can be together again."

The woman said as she choked back her tears, "I will never forgive you, and as far as us being together again, that will never happen either." When the woman finished speaking, she slammed the phone down on its hook and the two little love birds flew off and landed on a branch in a tall tree.

Drake said, "The woman is so mad at the other person that she cannot see past her own anger to appreciate the person she is talking to."

Daisy replied, "This is true. The person that the woman is mad at obviously means less to her than her own feelings, because she would rather stay mad than love and forgive."

As the two little love birds sat in the tree pondering the behavior of humans, a car came to a screeching halt.

"Get out of the road you dummies or I'll call the police," yelled the driver at a group of teens who were out in the road playing street ball.

"Ah, buzz off, or we'll play street ball on your car," replied the boys as they laughed and made motions as though they were jumping at the man.

"You haven't heard the last from me," threatened the old man as he sped off down the road.

"My goodness," said Daisy. "Humans are not very polite to each other."

"No, they aren't," said Drake. "But how can they be when they do not love each other. When you love someone, you will be nice to them, because they are very important to you."

"If only we could tell them how to love," Daisy said, as though there was no hope left for the human race.

"That's it," Drake said to Daisy with a huge smile on his face. "We will show the humans how to love," Drake added as he flew a spiral in the air.

Chapter Three: Love on Stage

Drake flew down and caught a shiny bottle cap off the ground and then he and Daisy flew over to where the girls were arguing. As they landed on the windowsill, the girls' attention was turned to the birds.

"Look," said one of the little girls. "It's two little love birds on our window sill and one of them has a bottle cap in its beak."

As the children watched, Drake held the bottle cap in his beak as Daisy danced around him, pecking at the cap.

The other child said, "It looks as though the bird without a cap wants the bird with the cap to share it."

"It sure does," said the other as they watched to see what would happen next.

Once Drake saw that the children understood what Daisy wanted, he leaned over and placed the cap on the sill in front of Daisy. Daisy chirped out a thank you, and then she leaned over and picked the cap up. The little girls looked at each other with wide eyes and open mouths, for they almost could not believe what they had just seen. Drake chirped out a "let's leave," and the two little love birds flew away and watched the girls from a limb in a nearby tree.

"The two little love birds sure love each other to share what little they have and not fight about it," said one of the girls with her head down in shame.

"Yeah," said the other little girl. "We should share our toys like the two little love birds did."

Just then one of the girls reached over and grabbed the doll they had been fighting over and gave it to the other girl. Then the girl who was getting the doll chirped like the love bird did and took the doll into her arms. They began making chirping noises and flapping their arms and they told all their friends about what they had been taught by the two little love birds.

Then Daisy and Drake flew over to the woman's house and upon their approach, Drake scooped up a flower out of the hanging basket.

The woman, still in tears, heard the birds chirping and turned to watch them.

"Oh, look," the woman said out loud to herself, "two adorable love birds."

Drake bounded over to Daisy and began to rub his shoulder up against hers. Then Drake hopped over to his freshly picked flower and offered it to Daisy. Daisy chirped out another thank you, then took the flower from Drake and the two little love birds hugged for a long time.

"This is the most romantic thing I think I have ever seen in my entire life," the woman said with tears streaming down her cheeks. She remembered when she got flowers from her mate. As she thought of those days of love and romance, her mind drifted to the fight she had just had with her husband. "Oh, no," said the woman in a shocked voice. "I just chased love away." The woman picked up the phone and called her husband and said, "A little bird told me that you still love me," and the husband told her of his unfailing love for her. The phone conversation ended with the couple reuniting, so Drake and Daisy flew off to where the boys were playing street ball.

The two little love birds waited and soon enough, the man in the car was coming back from the store that he went to earlier when he had his not-so-nice run in with the boys.

"Okay," Daisy alerted Drake. "What we need to do is get the old man to slow down long enough to meet the kids."

"Right," said Drake, "and I have the perfect plan." Drake whispered the plan into Daisy's ear and then they flew into action. As one of the boys hit the ball, both of the love birds caught it together and flew it over to where the old man had stopped at a stop sign.

"Look out below," laughed the two little love birds as they flew back to the tree.

"Hey," asked the old man angrily, "what's the meaning of you almost hitting me with your ball?"

"We didn't do it, Mister," the boys said honestly.

"No?" asked the old man. "Then who did?"

"It was those two little love birds that are watching us from the tree," the boys answered back.

"Will you throw us our ball so we can go back to playing?" one of the boys asked.

"I would," said the old man with a grin, "but none of you look like you know how to catch."

"Fire it in here, old man, and we'll show you a thing or two," one of the boys said as he took the catcher's position.

The old man wound up and released a blazing knuckle ball that sank right into the mitt of the boy who was waiting for it.

"Ouch," said the boy as he bounced around a bit.

"Man alive," one of the other boys confessed, "I've never seen a ball do what yours just did."

"Is that right?" the old man asked with a sparkle in his eyes. "I used to pitch in my younger days and I still have the arm to do it today."

"You sure do," the boys all agreed in amazement.

"Could you teach us how to be better baseball players?" one of the boys begged.

"I tell you what I'll do," said the old man. "If you will get off the street and play at the park, I'll meet you there in the afternoons and teach you what I know. Is that a deal?" inquired the old man as he held out his arms for a group hug.

"Oh, man, is it ever," the boys said all together in jubilant voices as they ran up to the old man and began hugging and patting him on the shoulders.

Chapter Four: Final Exam

Drake turned to Daisy and said, "We did good today."

"Yes we did, and I'm confident that everybody learned important lessons to live by," Daisy responded as she sat next to Drake.

"Oh, really?" Drake asked. "And what do you think the girls learned?"

"Well," Daisy said, "I believe that the little girls learned that things aren't nearly as important as the people around them. I think that they learned that loving means sharing and that sharing means giving, without counting the cost. Now that I answered your question, my darling, perhaps you would answer mine?"

"Sure," Drake said. "Ask me anything."

"Okay," Daisy continued. "What do you think the unforgiving woman learned today?"

"I think," Drake said, "that the woman learned that sometimes she could be right herself, but she was being wrong toward others. I think the woman learned that loving always means forgiving and that part of forgiving is forgetting those things that were wrongly done against her."

"So what should we conclude about the boys and the old man?" Drake asked Daisy.

"It seems to me," Daisy responded, "that both the boys and the old man didn't understand who the other person was."

"Yes," said Drake. "They also learned that loving isn't only done to those we already know, but it is for those we don't know as well. It is a well known truth that every friend we have was once a stranger we didn't know."

"Indeed, my love," said Daisy as she fluttered her wings. Then Daisy asked Drake, "What did you learn from us today, my dearest?"

"I learned that even the smallest of creatures can show and teach others about love," Drake said and then asked, "and what is it you learned, my love?"

Daisy snuggled up to Drake and then replied, "I learned that love isn't just a word that you say, but it's something that you truly feel and do toward others."

As the sun began to fade out of sight, two little love birds sat on a branch; one was Drake and the other one was Daisy. They finished their day singing about those things that they liked doing or about those whom they loved.

The Good Hearted Burglar

Chapter One: Unappreciated

"These kids are driving me crazy," said Joan.

"I know exactly what you mean," said Rick, her husband. "Why did we ever decide to be foster parents?"

Joan moaned out, "So we could have access to all of the government assistance we are getting for having them, you blockhead."

"Oh, yeah," Rick mumbled to himself. "Well, what should we do with them today?" Rick yelled back to Joan, who was in the other room. "I mean, we whipped them pretty good this morning for making a mess during breakfast. The last thing we need is for somebody to notice all the bruises and belt stripes we put on them."

"Yeah, you're right," Joan responded as she thought for a moment. "Let's just lock them inside the closet until we get back from work; that way they won't wander off to the neighbors and show them what they got for being bad."

"Okay," Rick said as he finished tying his tie. "I'll go and get one of their beach pails and a roll of toilet paper so they don't make a mess on the floor," Rick continued as he headed to the garage.

Joan went down the hall to her foster children's room and took them by the arms.

"Please quit squeezing my arm so hard," said little Elizabeth. "You're hurting me."

"Stop your squawking," Joan snapped back. "You're lucky I'm in a hurry or I would have spanked you for your rudeness just now. Now go into the closet if you know what's good for you."

Little Elizabeth went in without any resistance, glad to get away from Joan.

Thomas, on the other hand, struggled against Joan and said, "I don't want to go in there."

Joan, completely impatient with the children, slapped Thomas in the face so hard that it sent him sliding onto the closet floor.

As Thomas lay on the floor crying, Rick ran over and said as he was pushing Thomas further into the closet with his feet, "See what you get for being a smart mouth, you crybaby. Now, don't make a mess on our floor while you're in there or you'll get worse than that when we get home."

Joan was still enraged at Thomas for struggling with her, so she said to him in a stern tone, "You'll learn to mind me, young man, or you'll spend the rest of your life in the dark." With that warning, Joan giggled to herself as she turned the lights out to the closet and locked the door with a padlock.

Rick honked the horn and yelled out of the car window, "Hurry up, before you make us late for work," and then he backed the car out of the garage.

Joan quickly locked the house door, slammed the garage door closed, and rushed into the car. As Joan and Rick sped off to make it to work on time, the children huddled together, desperately afraid of the dark.

"Thomas," Elizabeth said, "I'm scared."

Thomas replied, "I am, too. But you know what?"

"What?" asked Elizabeth.

As Thomas hugged his little sister he said, "I'm more afraid of Joan and Rick getting mad at us than I am of being in the dark."

"Yeah, me too," Elizabeth said.

Chapter Two: Look What We Have Here

Charlie was a good ol' Irish boy, if ever there was one. He was just the most lovable and joyful person you could ever want to meet. Charlie had only one real flaw, which was that he liked stealing from the rich and giving to the poor — namely himself.

For a week now, Charlie had been on a stakeout, watching the daily routines of Joan and Rick. He did this because he planned on burglarizing their home soon and wanted to make sure he arrived when they were just leaving. He figured that it was a safe place to do some taking because Joan and Rick lived alone and on the few times he followed them to the grocery store, he never heard them make any mention of the children, nor did he ever see the children with them. Ever since the children moved in, they were not allowed to play in the front yard, so as far as Charlie was concerned, today was a good day to steal from the rich and give to himself.

All the houses in the area had high privacy fences surrounding them, which blocked out the view of the other homes. Charlie felt that the alley approach would be the best way to get inside the house. He parked his car down the alley a short distance away and strolled over to the back yard where he found the gate ajar. He got to the back door of the house and with a bit of skill, opened the locked door. Charlie gave out an Irish smile as he opened the door and walked into the house as though he just bought the place.

"Ah," Charlie said to himself, "it looks as though the luck of the leprechauns is still with ya. Now, let me eyes see what the pot is filled with today."

Charlie rummaged around the kitchen a bit, eating some doughnuts that were on the counter. He walked a little way down the hall when he came to the closet and saw that it had a padlock keeping it safe. "Ah, yes, here it is: the pot of gold they've been hiding and it has a lid on it." Charlie placed his wrecking bar inside the latch and jerked it. The lock tore from the door and the wall, sounding as though it weighed a ton as it fell to the ground. Charlie danced a little jig to celebrate the ease of his efforts that day.

Charlie switched on the lights, opened the door, and there to his surprise were Thomas and his little sister, Elizabeth.

"Please don't hurt us!" the children cried out.

Charlie reached up to scratch his head and said, "Look what we have here. Two little pups with beating marks all over them." Charlie continued as he stooped down closer to them, "I promise never to hurt you two. Will you make me a promise back?"

"What's that?" Thomas inquired.

"Promise me you won't scream so we can talk to each other," Charlie asked with a kind Irish voice.

"Deal," Thomas said, still holding his sister.

Charlie began his questioning by saying, "Tell me, lad, who done you and your sis this way?"

Thomas said in a whisper, "It was our foster parents."

Charlie continued by saying, "Now, tell me this: what could you and the lass here have done to anger them so mightily?"

Elizabeth liked Charlie's voice and wanting to talk with him spoke up and said, "We spilled milk while we were eating cereal."

"Ah, the little princess has a voice as sweet as the angel's there in heaven," Charlie said to comfort her.

Elizabeth gave him a big smile when she heard his compliment and accent, so she asked out of turn, "Are you a burglar?"

Charlie struggled for a moment with his eyes dancing some and then said enthusiastically, "Ah, little sister, I am, but a good-hearted burglar, I am."

"A good-hearted burglar," laughed Thomas. "What in the world is that?"

"I thought you'd be asking me that, sonny, so I want you to know that unlike most burglars who steal people's property, I only take little children who are being mistreated to my home where I take care of them until we can find a safe place for them to live," Charlie said, quite proud of his ingenuity.

"Wow," said Elizabeth. "We are being mistreated here, Charlie."

"I know that, child; that's why I'm here to save you two," Charlie said as he stood up and placed his hand on his hips.

"Cool," said Thomas. "Are you really going to take us away from here?"

Charlie smiled and said as joyfully as he could, "Yes, indeed, me boy, but I need you two to do me one favor."

"Oh, what is it Mr. Good-Hearted Burglar," Elizabeth said as she sprang to her feet.

"I'm going to need you to trust me until I can find you a decent home," Charlie said, and then sticking his hands out toward them, he finished bargaining by asking, "Is that a deal?"

The children leaped toward him and shook his hands and then gave him a big, overwhelming hug.

Chapter Three: All Points Bulletin

Joan and Rick finally made it back home that afternoon. They immediately went to the closet to see if a mess was made on their floor. In shock, they discovered that the lock had been broken and the children were gone. Joan was the first to realize that the children were not only missing, but taken.

"Look," Rick said, "the gate near the alley is open."

Joan's eyes brightened up as she asked, "Do you know what this means?"

"Yeah, I know what this means," Rick said in total confusion. "It means that we got ripped off."

"No, blockhead, this is the answer we've been waiting for," Joan continued with a giant smile on her face.

Rick, now more confused than ever, asked, "In what way does this help us? The children are loose and we have a messed up house."

"Think about it, you of few brain cells," Joan said. "Someone came and took the brats away from us. Whoever did this broke into our house. That makes that person an outlaw, which in turn means that nothing that person says can be trusted."

"So?" Rick inquired.

Joan slapped Rick in the face and then said, "You're worse than Thomas. I should have locked you up in the closet today as well, so that when I got home you would have been gone, too."

"But honey," Rick said sadly.

Joan said, "Think of it like this: we now have someone we can say put those belt marks on the children."

"Sure, I got it now," Rick said as though he had just figured out the secret to the black hole. "The burglar did it." Rick sat on the sofa and said, "Oh, yes-sir-ree-Bobby, we can call the police and report the break-in and inform them that our children were kidnapped. There's only one flaw with this story, though."

"What's that?" Joan inquired.

"Well, how do we explain that the children were here alone and that we had them locked up in the closet?" Rick questioned quite intelligently.

"Now you are using your head, my love," Joan said somewhat impressed with his momentary burst of brain power. Then Joan went into the kitchen and took a skillet from the hanger, walked back into the den and placed herself behind Rick, who was comfortably sitting in the recliner.

Joan sweetly called out to Rick, saying, "Dimples."

As Rick turned toward the intoxicating voice of his wife, Joan plowed into him with the skillet, scoring a direct hit in the forehead.

Rick flew up out of the recliner with a scream, as he angrily questioned Joan, "What in the world are you doing? Have you gone insane?"

Joan, holding the skillet like a tennis racket, exhaled as though she was releasing a big puff of smoke, and then said with a cynical look on her face, "Thank you, dearest, for using your head twice today."

"What do you mean by that?" Rick inquired, still holding his head.

"I mean that the burglar hit you in the head and knocked you out, and then he broke into the closet where we kept our family heirlooms worth tens of thousands of dollars. Then after he packed it all away, he went into the children's room while they were taking their nap and he nabbed them."

"Wow," Rick confessed, "even I believe that story." Rick walked into the kitchen and started to get some ice to put on his head.

"What are you doing, you idiot?" Joan asked alarmed.

"I'm trying to shrink the swelling a little bit, if you don't mind," Rick responded still agitated that Joan clobbered him.

"Yes, I do mind," Joan said as she took his ice-filled hand and lowered it away from his head. "Let it swell so that it looks all the more believable."

The more Joan schemed, the more Rick was impressed with her devious methods.

"Okay," Joan said as though she was going step-by-step through a recipe, "now you can call the police and I'll cut the onions."

"Onions?" Rick asked with another lost look on his face.

"Yes, onions," Joan said. "You play the role of the injured father and I'll play the part of a teary-eyed mother who just discovered that the children of her dreams have just been kidnapped, her husband badly battered, the house broken into and made a wreck, and the family treasures stolen."

Rick looked at Joan in complete amazement and said, "I hope they find the children dead."

Joan laughed as she said, "Now that wasn't very nice to say."

Rick laughed back saying, "I know."

After the police were finished doing their investigation, Channel 12 news arrived and asked if they could run a story on it. Joan immediately seized upon the opportunity to become famous as she sat on the living room couch holding a picture of the children in front of her. During the interview, Joan made mention of the terrible destruction that the burglar had done to the gate and house and how impossible it would be to go to work because someone would have to stay by the phone in case a ransom call came in. She finished her interview with a tearful plea for financial assistance from the community.

Chapter Four: Forty Shades of Love

Charlie lived out on a parcel of land in the country. It had a large lawn that was filled with beautiful grass and a field that he grew nothing but clover in.

Once he and the kids entered the house, Charlie got the bath water ready. They noticed that Charlie had a beautiful Christmas tree set up.

"Charlie," little Elizabeth said.

"What's that, Lassie?" Charlie cheerfully asked.

"Could we see the Christmas tree lights?" Elizabeth continued.

"Oh, so you like sparkly lights, do you?" Charlie knowingly questioned.

As the children nodded their heads, Charlie lit up the Christmas tree and then turned on his most favorite song in the whole world, *Christmas in Killarney*. As the song played, Charlie began to dance and the children began to clap. Then, Elizabeth jumped onto the floor to see if she could dance to the song the way Charlie was doing it. Over and over, the song played and each time it played, the children got more involved with their clapping and dancing. Charlie went to his room and pulled out an instant camera with which he began taking pictures of his two new friends.

Thomas sat down and acted as though he hadn't slept in days.

"What's wrong, lad?" Charlie inquired.

"I'm hungry," Thomas complained.

"Do people your size eat peanut butter and jelly sandwiches?" Charlie said with a puzzled look as though he really didn't know.

"Oh, yes sir, we eat lots of peanut butter and jelly sandwiches," Thomas said as he sat up in his chair.

"Then come on, lad, and I'll set you up a round or two," Charlie said happily.

While they ate, the children were still kicking their legs from all the fun they were having listening to the music and watching Charlie jiggle as he made more sandwiches. Elizabeth accidentally kicked the table, causing her to spill some of her milk. Thomas froze in fear of what just happened because he remembered the price they had paid earlier that day for the same mistake in front of their foster parents.

As Charlie said with a big smile on his face, "Oops, me little angel had the cloud pulled out from underneath her," he reached over and lovingly wiped her face with a damp towel and then wiped up the mess on the table.

Thomas and Elizabeth looked at each other with a smile on their faces and continued eating the best peanut butter and jelly sandwiches they had ever had.

Once the children finished eating, Charlie had them take baths and get dressed for bed. Before they went to bed, though, Charlie sat on the couch with them and read them a short story of an Irish prince and the noble things he did for others.

"That prince is you, Charlie," Elizabeth said as she leaned against his arms.

"Do you think so?" Charlie questioned back.

"Yes, indeed," said Thomas as Elizabeth was looking up and nodding her head.

"Well, I'll be having to believe you on that one, for I'm unsure of me own nobleness," Charlie said as he reached around both of them, giving them a hug of thanks for their kind words.

"Now, it's off to bed with you all, or there won't be no green on the grass by morning," Charlie said as though he believed there really was such a curse.

"Good night, Uncle Charlie," the children said as they smothered him with more big hugs.

"Ah, all right now, me dearest ones. Good night and sleep tight," Charlie said as he rushed them off to bed.

Charlie danced a little bit as he made his way back toward the den. Though he weighed a good 200 pounds, there was no doubt that he felt like he was walking on air. He had totally forgotten how it felt to be so useful to someone else and to feel their genuine love back to him. He sat down in front of the TV and turned it to Channel 12. The news was on and the main story was the kidnapping of the two children he saved. He watched the tearful interview that the evil stepmother gave.

"Ah, baloney," Charlie said in disgust as he listened. "The only thing that lady has missing is the broomstick she flew in on," Charlie continued saying to himself.

As Charlie sat watching the news, he realized that the record needed to be set straight. He decided that he would turn the children over to the police tomorrow, but tonight, he would make sure his little friends rested comfortably and safe.

Chapter Five: Setting the Record Straight

Charlie wanted to make sure that the children had the grandest of meals, so he made pancakes, eggs, bacon, biscuits with gravy, and if that didn't hit the spot, he also made blueberry muffins. The children were used to cold cereal, and when they saw all that Charlie cooked for them, they wasted no time loading their plates with everything. That morning, while the children slept, Charlie made good use of the time by washing and drying their clothes. After breakfast, Charlie got them dressed and took them out to his car, where he strapped them in and drove toward the police station.

"Where are we going, Charlie?" Thomas inquired.

"Well, lad, remember I told you at your house that I took children that were being abused in order to find them a better home?"

"Yes," Thomas said as he remembered their first conversation.

"That's where I'm taking you two, to get yourselves a better home to live in," Charlie said with a knot in his throat.

"But we found a better home with you, Charlie," Thomas said disappointingly.

Elizabeth just said in a long, aggravated tone, "Charlie."

Charlie knew what he had to do wouldn't be easy, but it was the only way to save the children from going back to their foster parents.

As Charlie stepped through the door at the police station with a child in each hand, Officer McGregor announced to the crew, "Look what we have here: O'Riley has come for a visit and he's toting two wee pups."

"McGregor, I thought you died," Charlie said back with a smile.

"I'm still waiting for the official report," replied Officer McGregor.

As the men in the office were laughing, it finally dawned on them who the children were.

"Hey, wait a minute now," Officer McGregor said as he waved his arms to everybody to settle down. "Aren't these here youngsters the missing children who were abducted?"

"We're not missing," Elizabeth said, causing the officers standing around to gawk a little in amusement.

"Well then," Officer McGregor said, "it seems you are right, little one. Where did O'Riley find you wandering around?"

"In the closet," Thomas said, so he could join the conversation that was going on.

"In the closet?" McGregor asked, confused.

"I can explain," Charlie said as he tried to put his hand over Thomas's mouth.

Pulling Charlie's hand away from his mouth, Thomas continued talking by adding, "Yes, indeed, Charlie is the good-hearted burglar."

At that, Charlie knew the game was up and instead of trying to fish his way out of it, he simply turned as he gave everybody a look of shear embarrassment.

"I'll be calling Child Protective Services while Officer Muldoon assists the children over to the break room," McGregor said as he motioned his head at Muldoon toward the children. "As for you, Charlie, we will need to take your picture over in the print room so you can get your reward."

Charlie knew what that meant, so he bent down on his knees and took the children in his arms and hugged them tightly. "I need you two to make me another promise," Charlie said.

"What's that?" the children asked together.

"I need you to promise me," continued Charlie, "that you will be nice to Officer Muldoon and let him show you to your new home. Will you do that for me while I go to the other room with Officer McGregor?"

"Yes," the children said sadly.

As Charlie rose to go into the fingerprinting room, you could see a stream of tears flowing from his eyes. The men were obviously disturbed when they saw this, for no one had ever seen anything but a smile on Charlie's face. Charlie was careful not to allow the children to see him crying as they went their separate ways.

Before the mug shot and fingerprints were taken, Charlie was asked to empty his pockets and to place the contents on the table. As he emptied his overall pockets, he removed the instant pictures that he took of the children the day before. The investigator looked hard at them and raced out of the room. Charlie heard some raised voices, but could not make them out. Officer McGregor accompanied the detective when he came back in.

"Tell us, Charlie," McGregor said insistently, "did you find the children all bruised up like this at their house?"

"Ay, I did," Charlie said, still wiping tears from his eyes.

The detective jumped in at that point and said, "Charlie, we know you were robbing the house when you came upon the children, but what we don't know is where you found them when you took them away."

Charlie, realizing what was going on, said with one of his eyebrows raised, "I can see here, gentlemen, that you are in need of an eyewitness to a possible abuse case and as you can see, I'm in need of a plea bargain."

The detective and McGregor stepped out of the room for a moment and came back in. McGregor said, "Tell us what we need to know and I'll see what I can do to help you out in court. I'm not making any promises that the judge will go easy on you, Charlie, but I'm giving you my word, I will mention your cooperation." McGregor stuck out his hand and Charlie clasped onto it stating, "You got yourself a deal."

Chapter Six: What a Fine Mess This Is

After receiving the testimony from Charlie about how he discovered the children, Joan and Rick were immediately picked up and charged with felony counts of child endangerment, battery, and abuse. Due to the fact that this was committed against foster children, the judge threw the book at them.

It was Charlie's time now, and Channel 12 news was there to get the full story. Bets were going on all over the county on what the judge would do to him. Charlie pleaded guilty to the burglary charge and then sat back down to await his sentence.

Officer McGregor and the detective asked if they could approach the bench and the judge motioned for them and there they held a low-toned discussion. A few times, the judge would move his head around in order to look at Charlie. As this was going on, the new foster parents of Thomas and Elizabeth came through the door, holding the children by their hands. Charlie's attorney noticed them entering and got up to meet them. As the attorney began shaking the foster parents' hands, the children saw Charlie sitting in the front, so they shouted out, "Charlie!" Thomas and Elizabeth tore loose from the grips of their foster parents and ran up to the front where Charlie was. When they got close enough, they jumped into his arms where they began laughing hysterically from the joy of finally being back together.

The courtroom erupted with noise as people began sharing their comments with each other. Channel 12 was videotaping the entire spectacle and feeding it live to the station down the street. Every business in town had a TV on and everyone in the area was watching the case as it unfolded.

The judge used his gavel to regain the court's composure and then said, "The court has arrived at a decision. Would the accused stand?"

Charlie placed the children gently on their feet and taking one in each hand, Charlie stood facing the judge.

The judge continued as he gave his verdict and sentence, "On examining all of the evidence, the court finds Charlie Maxwell O'Riley guilty of burglary of a habitation. Notwithstanding, and due to unusual circumstances, the court finds it necessary to take into consideration the cooperation of the accused in how such cooperation from him assisted the efforts of law enforcement officials in concluding a case of serious magnitude. The court has determined that the accused be given one year probation and a fine of two thousand dollars, plus court costs and attorney fees. Also, due to the nature of the case and the good-heartedness that the accused has consistently demonstrated toward the children involved in the earlier mentioned case, the court has determined that it can find no reason why Charlie Maxwell O'Riley should be restricted from visiting Thomas and Elizabeth, so long as such visitations are permitted by the managing conservators who are in charge of said children. This case is closed and the court is now out of session."

With that, the audience within the courtroom jumped to their feet cheering and applauding. Charlie took the children in his arms and hopped around the courtroom a bit as he danced another Irish jig with them.

"Charlie," Elizabeth said.

"What's that, princess?" Charlie inquired with a giant smile on his face.

"Can we go to your place and turn the Christmas lights on?" Elizabeth asked.

"Sure we can," Charlie said. "And if you'd like, we can dance and eat peanut butter and jelly sandwiches."

"All right!" Thomas shouted, as they left laughing and dancing all the way into the street.

Last Man Standing

Chapter One: Agitation Bugs

"Make way, tubby," Prissy said as she nudged Delmar with her elbow and hips.

"Oh, Prissy, I see you are just as polite and kind as usual," Delmar said as he side-stepped a little to give Prissy room at the coffee machine.

"Look, Delmar, you know that unhealthy looking people really agitate me," Prissy said as she poured herself a cup of coffee. "I mean, my gosh, Delmar, just look at how big you've gotten. You remind me of a prehistoric blowfish, big and round." Prissy snickered at her ingenuity in putting her ideas together in a humorous way.

Delmar reached into his pocket and acted as though he had something in his hand. "I agitate you?" Delmar inquired. "You might be surprised to learn that I found an agitation bug this morning. Here, take a look," Delmar said as he took his hand out of his pocket and opened it just in front of Prissy's face.

"I don't see anything but your empty, chubby hand, Delmar," Prissy said, somewhat agitated.

"Look closer, Prissy," Delmar said raising his hand a little closer to her eyes.

"Look, super-size-it, there isn't a thing in your hand," Prissy said, even more agitated than she was before.

Delmar asked with a big smile on his face and a hearty laugh, "You see why they call it an agitation bug? It already has you getting mad."

"Oh, that does it, Delmar," Prissy said stammering for self-composure. "Just wait and see how agitated you get when I get the Asian market and all you wind up with is Bermuda. While I'm shopping till I'm dropping, empire style, you'll still be over here struggling with your eating disorder."

"Get real," Delmar said as he rolled his eyes to suggest to Prissy that she was in a daze. Then raising a napkin, Delmar started fanning

Prissy's face as though she were suffering from heat exhaustion and added, "Surely you don't think that you are going to be the one chosen to do all of the buying for Raven Industries in Asia this year?"

Prissy began jabbing her long fingernails into Delmar's stomach as she said enthusiastically, "Contrary to what you can envision, Menu Man, I have a hunch that the best candidate for the job will be the best looking candidate to choose from — me!" With that proclamation, Prissy spun on her heels and headed off to the conference room where the purchasing agents were assembling. During this meeting, they would learn what territories they would be assigned to work for the coming year's product acquisitions.

As Delmar watched Prissy voluptuously walk away, he grew somewhat concerned about what she had just said because every purchasing agent wanted that assignment.

Carlton the maintenance man came over to Delmar and said, "The big honcho wants you in his office right now."

Delmar arrived at Mr. Tyson's office wearing the biggest, I'm-happy-with-my-job smile he could muster.

Mr. Tyson was the owner of Raven Industries and looked stern faced as he said, "Delmar, it has been brought to my attention that one of my employees has been insulting you every morning at the coffee machine and throughout the day. Is that true?"

"Well, ah, yes, that would be true, sir," Delmar said as his smile seemed to fall from his face and shatter into a million pieces.

"I'll need to make an example out of her to the rest of the company," Mr. Tyson said as he looked out his window onto the city below. He continued by asking Delmar, "Would you like to be in the office when she gets her termination papers?"

"You mean, fire Prissy?" Delmar said, shocked at what he was hearing.

"Yes, Prissy. I intend to fire Miss Shoemaker before the hour is out," Mr. Tyson said with increasing passion.

"No, Mr. Tyson, please, don't fire her," Delmar said in a distressed plea. "If you fire her, you'll have to fire me as well."

Mr. Tyson turned around and asked, "You mean to tell me that as mean-spirited as she has been toward you, that you will not retaliate against her and make her suffer for how she has made you suffer?"

"That's right, Mr. Tyson," Delmar said, still shaking from fear of what might happen next.

"Very well then, Delmar, I'm glad I heard that personally from you," Mr. Tyson said with a sneaky look on his face. "Actually, I have a special assignment for you to do for me this year and I needed to know that you weren't vindictive toward people who insult you."

"Not in the least, Mr. Tyson," Delmar said with a newly constructed smile on his face.

"Good, son. Now, make your way to the conference room and I'll be there shortly," Mr. Tyson said as he pointed Delmar toward the door.

At the conference room, old man Tyson came in and closed the door. With a warm smile, he turned and looked at each employee as he made his way to the head of the table located at the other end of the room. Everyone liked working for him, because it was like being near their own beloved grandfather. He had an old kind of style and charm that was flavored with a good dose of southern fried hospitality, which made the ladies melt and the men jealous with envy. As he made his way to the end of the table, the sales agents randomly called out to him, "Hi, Mr. Tyson" or "Mr. Tyson, sir." He would elegantly answer back to his greeters, "Good day, sweet lady," or to the men he would say, "Greetings, dear boy." His rustic accent along with his aged voice put everyone at ease and no one spoke because Mr. Tyson had the kind of voice you could listen to for hours and never get tired of hearing it.

Mr. Tyson began the meeting by saying, "Friends, we all know what today's meeting is all about. I've spent a great deal of time laboring over who is to work what zones for this year's purchasing needs. I have decided that our large Asian market needs to have two purchasers working it this year instead of the one that is typically utilized. Therefore, with that said, I have assigned both Prissy Shoemaker and Delmar Coppertone to work this area together. They will combine their talents and expertise to find for us the very best items that the American consumer will want to buy."

Upon that announcement, Prissy acted out to those watching as though she was overwhelmed with the news. As the other agents applauded her and Delmar for their prestigious assignment, Prissy, deep down, was having herself a secret shouting match. Delmar immediately realized what his special assignment from Mr. Tyson was.

Mr. Tyson continued the meeting by calling out the other agent's names; he gave each of them an envelope with their assigned territories and pertinent documents for those areas. He added as he was walking toward the exit, "If you have any need to talk with me concerning your assignments, I will be in my office for the next hour, before retiring for the rest of the day. Good day, all."

Delmar shot Prissy a quick, but not enthusiastic smile, for he knew just how close Prissy had come to getting fired. Prissy turned in disgust, unable to look at him.

When the meeting ended, everyone left in an excited rush to begin their new assignments. Delmar was the last person leaving the conference room except for Prissy who was still sitting dumbfounded in her chair. As Delmar reached the door, he turned to congratulate Prissy and said, "Prissy, I just wanted to tell you how glad I am to be working with such a capable person as you."

Prissy jumped to her feet leaning against the table and said, "Let me tell you something, happy hippo, I wouldn't spend time with you even if you were the last man standing. Got it?"

Delmar was shocked and disappointed, but he managed to hide it as he courteously responded back to her with, "Yeah. I got it."

As soon as everybody left the conference room, Prissy dashed over to Mr. Tyson's office. Just when Prissy knocked on the door, she heard Mr. Tyson's kind southern voice say, "Come in young lady, I've been expecting you. Oh, and do shut the door behind you."

Wasting no time with polite greetings, Prissy launched off into her most desperate anti-Delmar excuse speech she could muster. "Mr. Tyson, I beg you to reconsider your decision about sending Delmar to Asia with me. I don't think it is a good idea to send a person as unhealthy as he is into an area as rugged as the Orient."

Prissy continued her sermon with a greatly disturbed look upon her face as she said, "I mean, if he were to fall down and hurt himself, how could I get him up? And the cars are really small over there, so it would be impossible to move him from one manufacturer to the other without a lot of trouble."

Before Prissy could go any further, Mr. Tyson interrupted her with a wave of his hand and said, "I suppose if Menu Man were to fall down, he could eat enough of himself away, in order to be light enough for you to help lift him up."

"Uh oh," Prissy said turning red, "you heard me say that to

Delmar this morning?"

"Yes, Miss Shoemaker, I did," Mr. Tyson said with a disappointed look upon his face. "And sadly, if you want to know the truth, young lady, I've heard your violent assault against him every morning for the past year. You have run that man down for nothing more than being overweight, yet you never seemed to get upset with my weight situation. I can't remember one time when you've run me down because of it, but with Delmar you've gone the extra mile."

As Prissy began to open her mouth to say something, Mr. Tyson interrupted her again as he popped his hand upon his desk, saying, "Hang on now. I'm not through speaking."

Prissy jumped a little in fright. "Please continue, sir," Prissy said. "I didn't mean to interrupt you."

"Miss Shoemaker," Mr. Tyson said as he drew back in his chair, "I've thought long and hard about what I should do with you concerning your mistreatment of Delmar, and I thought you would make the perfect example in how our company doesn't tolerate discrimination or abuse. So, in preparation for this meeting, I had your pay calculated and your termination papers drawn up."

Prissy began shaking all over from fear that she was about to lose her job. "Yet," Mr. Tyson injected, "in time, it became clear to me that perhaps what we needed to show our fellow employees was an example of how people can learn to resolve their problems and be reconciled. So if you care to keep this job, then you will go to Asia with Delmar and you will treat him with common respect and human dignity. Hopefully, in the course of working together, you can learn to appreciate Delmar for who he is, and not for who he isn't according to your high, regal standards. Now, are these terms acceptable to you or should I have the human resources department bring me your pay and separation papers?"

Prissy was so ashamed of herself that she raised her hand to her mouth to cover it as she quietly wept. The whole ordeal of being placed with Delmar on a job assignment and then having one of the most beloved persons in her life speak sternly to her was more than she could bear.

Mr. Tyson seeing that he had upset Prissy, stood up and went around his desk. Sitting on its edge, he held out his arms and said in a gentle grandfatherly way, "Come here, my dear. I'm truly sorry that I've upset you." With that kind invitation, Prissy dove into Mr. Tyson's chest and cried out loud, apologizing for the way she had been acting.

Mr. Tyson covered the side of her head with his hand and said, "There, there, child, tomorrow can be a brand new day." After a few minutes, Mr. Tyson took a hanky from his pocket and gave it to Prissy saying, "Goodness, I do believe your face is melting." Prissy realized that he was speaking of her makeup running, laughed some as she dried her eyes. Her spirit calmed down as she found security in the arms of a man she admired and respected above all others.

"Now, before you leave me," Mr. Tyson added, "I'd like to hear you promise that you'll look after Delmar and help him succeed."

Prissy looked up into Mr. Tyson's blue eyes and said, "I promise, Mr. Tyson. I won't let you down again."

With that said, Mr. Tyson took Prissy by one of her hands and led her to the door. As Prissy stepped out of the office, Mr. Tyson said to her, "Would you be so kind as to keep me posted on how things are going over in Asia?"

Prissy nodded her head then turned to leave.

"Oh, and one more thing," Mr. Tyson added.

"What's that, sir?" Prissy asked.

Mr. Tyson looked Prissy dead in the eyes and lowly said so no one else could hear, "I gave Delmar the opportunity to pick your replacement this morning, because I told him that I was going to fire you sometime in the near future."

Prissy raised her eyebrows in a curious fashion and inquired, "Who did he chose to take my place?"

"I knew you'd want to know that," Mr. Tyson said with a wide smile. "Odd as it seems, he requested that I keep you."

"He did?" Prissy asked as she pondered his motives.

"As a matter of fact, Prissy," Mr. Tyson added, "he threatened me that if I fired you, I'd have to fire him as well."

Prissy gulped hard as she asked in amazement, "He did?"

"Yes, little lady, he did. And to think that he did that in spite of all he's been through with you. I found that to be a very noble thing for him to do. Don't you agree?" Mr. Tyson asked, as he ended the conversation by slowly closing the door behind her.

Prissy stood outside Mr. Tyson's office dazed from all that just happened. As she made her way to the elevator, she reached into her pocket for something and pulled out her hand. Raising her empty hand to her face she said, "There you are, you little devil. I had no idea you guys were so reproductive."

Carlton the maintenance man looked at Prissy in an odd way as he watched her enter the elevator with an empty hand opened in front of her face.

"What did you find there, Miss Shoemaker?" Carlton asked, gazing into her empty hand.

"An agitation bug," Prissy said as she closed her hand and shook it vigorously.

Before Carlton could find out what she meant, the elevator door closed, leaving him a bit agitated.

Chapter Two: Last Man Standing

"First class seating," Delmar said excitedly as he shot Prissy a smile.

Prissy gave him a thoughtful smile back as she said, "As far away as we are going for this assignment, you'd have thought they would have sent us on a cruise ship."

Delmar chuckled as he pondered her witty comment.

"You know, Delmar," Prissy continued, "I know that talking would make our trip go by faster, but we are going to suffer from jet lag by the time we get there if we don't get some rest. I promise you that when we land, I'll spend a bunch of time with you and we can talk till our jaws drop off. Is that a deal?"

Delmar was pleased to see how thoughtful and civil Prissy was being, so he replied, "Sounds like a deal to me."

Arriving in Japan, Prissy and Delmar took a small charter plane to one of their first scheduled stops located in the Philippines. Along with the pilot and co-pilot, there were two other passengers traveling with them: a female Asian model named Shezuka and her photojournalist, Tamahaki, who was actually cuter than the model she worked for. Everyone spoke English, which was a plus considering that the weather station reported that a serious storm was active in the area. The captain felt it could be avoided by flying over the top of the storm cell. Somewhere over the many hundreds of unexplored islands of the Philippines, the pilot announced, "Attention passengers; we are experiencing problems and are seeking a place to make an emergency landing. Please secure your personal items and fasten your seatbelts."

After the intercom went silent, words could still be heard coming from the cockpit. "Mayday, mayday, this is Charter Flight 3308. We are experiencing severe instrumentation malfunctions and are unsure of our heading and altitude. Requesting immediate clearance and emergency staff standing by upon our —"

Before the captain could finish his statement, the plane violently ripped its way into thick jungle foliage. The captain, not knowing what the actual altitude was, accidentally flew the plane into a canopy of trees. Luckily, they did not smash into the side of a mountain, but landed almost intact on the sandy floors of a tropical island. Only the wings and the cockpit sustained heavy damage.

All the passengers were uninjured. Everyone sat dazed in their seats, looking around as though they did not want to accept what had just happened.

"Delmar!" Prissy shouted.

"I'm okay; are you okay?" Delmar answered.

"I'm fine," Prissy replied as she began tossing herself against the exit door in an attempt to get it open. "Don't just sit there," she said as she continued tossing herself against the door. "Help me get it open."

Delmar reached down and lifted the door up and out with ease. Not wishing to make Prissy feel any worse than she already did, he said, "You must have loosened it up."

Prissy looked outside but didn't like what she saw. She turned back to Delmar and admitted, "Delmar, I'm really, really afraid."

Delmar held her arms as he tried to reassure her that he could handle the situation. The one thing he couldn't do was show any fear, for he knew that Prissy and the other passengers would need his strength in order to survive.

"Please, don't any of you ladies be afraid," Delmar kindly demanded. "I'm not sure how long we are going to be stuck out here, but it seems that the only way we are going to survive until we are found is to work together. Now I don't know what's outside this plane, but I promise you all that I will do all that I can to keep you safe. That's the best deal I can make under the circumstances."

Prissy was pleased to see how brave and serious Delmar was acting, so she responded with a supportive tone in her voice, "Good enough, Delmar."

Shezuka and Tamahaki both nodded their heads.

Entering the cockpit, they realized that the captain would be dead in the next few hours. The co-pilot was already dead.

"What are we going to do for the pilot," Tamahaki asked almost in tears.

"There's nothing we can do for him, Tamahaki," Delmar replied. "We're doomed if we do and doomed if we don't."

"What do you mean by that?" Shezuka inquired.

Delmar turned toward her and said, "The captain has several serious wounds internally, just looking at the amount of blood he has already spit up. I'm pretty sure that if we move him, we will only aggravate the wounds, which will cause him excruciating pain. As it stands, he is dying comfortably, but if we move him, he will die quicker and in a lot of pain."

"So what are you saying?" Tamahaki asked. "Are you saying that we stand by and let this man die?"

"As it stands, Tamahaki," Delmar said somewhat defensively, "he is semi-conscious and resting comfortably. We cannot stop the internal bleeding, but if we begin to move him, then he'll wake up from the pain we are causing him and he'll die regardless of where we move him."

Prissy jumped into the conversation in order to calm it down, for it was obvious to her that Delmar was growing increasingly uncomfortable having to explain his actions. "So," Prissy blurted out, "what do you propose we do next?"

Delmar turned to Prissy with a pale look and said, "I'll dig the graves; you girls start gathering fire wood. It might take me a while to get the hole ready, so if you finish before I get back, then begin taking inventory of what we have available inside the plane. We are going to need everything we can get our hands on."

Delmar exited the aircraft and found a piece of the wing that had been torn off from the crash. Knowing that in a few days the bodies would begin to smell, he wisely chose a location that was far away from their new home. Delmar hadn't worked that hard in years, but after two hours, the two holes were dug deep enough to take their occupants. Delmar placed the co-pilot first and after covering him in sand, began gathering stones in order to seal the grave off from small creatures that might want to disturb it.

Entering the plane, Delmar went over and checked on the captain. He was now dead and Delmar was glad that he — not one of the women — had found him this way. He knew it would be hard on them and so at every chance that he could lessen the hardship, he would.

The captain was buried alongside his co-pilot and as Delmar was gathering stones with what little energy he had left, Shezuka approached Delmar and said, "Well, it looks like you are the last man standing."

Delmar quickly passed through his mind what Shezuka said and all that it meant and then as he was collapsing to the ground from exhaustion, he said back to her, "That's what I am, the last man standing."

Chapter Three: Snake, Rattle, and Roll

Being the only man on an island with three women had its advantages. Though all of them worked hard in putting their camp together, Delmar was always the one who had to do the jobs that required the most labor and strength. He didn't mind, though, for he felt useful and important.

One night, the camp had a survivor's meeting to discuss their plight and to determine the best course of survivability. Shezuka seemed to like taking charge, for she was used to ordering Tamahaki around. "Tamahaki, go to the plane and get my knapsack," Shezuka said as she always did.

"Get it yourself," Tamahaki replied to her.

Shezuka couldn't believe what she heard and said in a bitter tone, "What did you just tell me?"

Tamahaki said, "I said to go get it yourself."

Shezuka rose to her feet and said something back to her sternly in their native tongue, then stomped off toward the plane.

Prissy jumped in again and said, "Well, Tamahaki, it's good to have you working full time for the camp."

As the three smiled, a friendship was forged between them.

Once Shezuka made her way back to the fire, Delmar began a meeting he wanted to have days ago, but never got around to it.

"Ladies," Delmar said as he quickly looked at each of the girls, "I'm not sure how long we will be here, but we do know we have been here for two days and haven't heard a single plane pass by. That means something is wrong with the plane's beacon. We need to assign duties in order that our daily needs are met. Who would like to be responsible for gathering the wood so we can keep the fire going?" Everybody knew that wood gathering was a demanding job and so no one volunteered.

"We'll need to draw straws for it then," Delmar said as he began snapping twigs in his hands.

As he held out his hand, each lady drew their straw and then he asked them to show the others what they drew. Shezuka drew the short stick and instantly demanded a rematch.

"Save your breath, I'll do it," Tamahaki said as she reclined in her hollowed-out sand chair.

"That's very nice of you to do this for us, Tamahaki," Delmar said as he gave her a look of admiration.

"Okay then, that leaves food gathering and food cooking," Delmar said as he held out two new sticks.

"The food gatherer will draw the shortest stick," Delmar said as he threw the rest of his sticks in the fire.

Shezuka drew the food cooking stick and was quick to ask, "And what about you, Delmar, don't you work around here anymore?"

Delmar, being the patient man that he is, kindly told her, "I will be the builder, the hunter, and the explorer. I get three jobs to each of your one and these jobs are always mine."

Shezuka calmed down and accepted her role when she realized she didn't have it as bad as the rest.

Delmar made himself busy constructing makeshift hammocks so they could sleep off the ground and he also made a pen to store firewood material. He made plates and bowls out of the plane's sheet metal. The plane itself was their storage shed, which held what little implements they had and their food.

One day, as Delmar was scouting out the area to see if it was safe for Prissy to forage for food, a large boa moved its way down out of a tree and quickly wrapped itself around Delmar.

Delmar screamed, "Stay back!"

Prissy was in a state of alarm and not sure what to do, so she instinctively picked up a large stick and began batting away at the serpent. Strike one, Delmar screamed from her blow. Strike two, and Delmar screamed again. Strike three, and Delmar shouted out to her, "Woman, what in the blazes are you trying to do — help the snake!?"

Prissy snickered as she realized how comical Delmar was under such tremendous pressure.

Delmar yelled like an Apache warrior as he ran straight for a coconut tree. The tree rattled from the force of the snake slamming into it. Obviously the trick worked for the snake loosened its grip and Delmar hit the ground and rolled his way out of it. Delmar picked up his homemade ax and killed the man-eater.

Sitting down for a well-deserved rest, Delmar looked up at Prissy and said, "Ever ate snake meat before?"

Prissy landed on the ground next to Delmar and laughed hysterically as she took his head into her hands and said, "No, Delmar, I haven't, but thanks to you, it looks like tonight will be my lucky night."

Prissy, for the first time, looked intently into Delmar's dark blue eyes and liked what she saw in them.

She asked Delmar with a smirk on her face, "Do you think that Shezuka knows how to clean and cook python?" Delmar burst into laughter with Prissy as they enjoyed the thought of what was in store for their cook.

Prissy stood on her feet, then extended her hands to Delmar, saying, "Come on, big man, it's the last dance of the day and I feel like cutting the rug."

Delmar was thrilled to see Prissy so playful and at ease around him and taking her by the hands, he stood up and then embraced her, asking, "You know what the perfect song would be considering what we just went through?"

"Tell me, for I haven't a clue," Prissy giggled.

As Delmar swung her around in a circle he said, "I think the appropriate request from us should be, *Snake, Rattle, and Roll.*"

"Oh ho, Delmar," Prissy laughed again. "That is the perfect request," she said as she leaned her head upon his shoulder and swayed to the imaginary music.

Prissy and Delmar became true friends from that moment on and love began to grow like the jungle they now called home.

Chapter Four: Spin the Bottle

Two months later, the survivors were quite proficient in their daily tasks. Delmar lost most of his extra weight and had become quite the male specimen. Shezuka, wanting Delmar for herself, decided she would attempt to cause a rift between Prissy and Delmar.

As they were eating their evening meal, under the light of a full moon and campfire, Shezuka asked, "Is there any reason why we have to stay bored-to-tears while we're stuck in this jungle?" Everybody looked around a bit at each other and then Tamahaki asked, "What do you have in mind?"

Shezuka responded with her well-devised answer, "Well, I was just thinking that perhaps we could play spin the bottle in order to help us pass the time. It would also help us get to know each other a little better."

Tamahaki, not realizing the craftiness behind Shezuka's request, said, "Wow, that is a really good idea. I'm in."

"Sounds like fun. I'm in also," Delmar said.

Prissy was not so thrilled about it because she had played this game before in the past and knew how personal it could get.

Tamahaki went to the plane and took out a used shampoo bottle and filled it with sand. "The lid will be the pointer," she said. "And whoever it falls closest to will have to truthfully answer a question from the rest of us."

Shezuka was secretly laughing to herself at how easily this was working out for her. She thought to herself, *this is why I hired Tamahaki, because she is so gullible.*

Tamahaki spun the bottle and it rolled closest to Prissy. Prissy bit her lip in an attempt to hide her dissatisfaction.

Just as Shezuka was about to launch into her divide-and-conquer questions, Tamahaki took the lead and asked, "If you could eat anything in the world right now, what would it be?"

Prissy was relieved to get such a question and then said, "I think under the circumstances, that it would have to be a buffet setting where I could eat all the meatloaf and mashed potatoes I could load up on."

Everybody laughed at her reply, and then Delmar asked, "If you could have just one thing air dropped to us, what would it be?"

Prissy, realizing how funny her first answer was, said, "I would have the entire restaurant that has the buffet line dropped down just over there so we could all pig out."

Prissy calculated her response correctly because it made them laugh harder.

Then, Shezuka came to the mound and fired in a curve ball question that took the happy group from joyful bliss to quiet concern: "So, tell me, Prissy, have you and Delmar always been such good friends or is this just because he lost all the fat and now is good enough for you?"

Delmar, not believing what Shezuka just said, turned to Prissy and said, "You don't have to answer that kind of a question."

"And why not?" Shezuka demanded. "Her not answering the question will only prove that she thought you were a disgusting pig before we crash-landed. It's true, isn't it, Prissy? You only began to like Delmar after he shed all of his fat and not before."

Prissy, her eyes welling up with tears turned to Delmar and said, "Shezuka is somewhat right. At first I did not appreciate the person that Delmar is, simply because of his excess weight. I was so busy judging him based upon his physical imperfections that I never came to appreciate his good nature and kind heart."

As Delmar was about to offer his words of comfort and support, Shezuka jumped in again with another question: "So how long have you known Delmar, anyway?"

Still in some form of moderate shock, Prissy tearfully said, "Seventeen months."

Tamahaki, seeing how upset Prissy was being made, prepared herself to punch Shezuka in the face. Delmar, realizing the facial expression and manner of her movements, reached over to her and said, "Please don't."

Dropping back to her seat, Tamahaki sat with a disgusted look on her face at Shezuka.

"My, my," Shezuka said with a look of disbelief, "seventeen months and you never realized who Delmar really was, and now fifty-five pounds later, you can?"

"Lay off," Tamahaki shouted, "or I'll lay you out!"

Shezuka stood up and screamed back, "You would attack me to

cover up the truth about what kind of a person Prissy really is!"

Tamahaki, unsure how to respond to Shezuka's response, turned and stared into the darkness of the jungle.

"That's right," Shezuka said in her new wave of accusations. "Turn away like she's been doing for the past seventeen months. Even though it's obvious to us all just how cold and cruel she's been toward Delmar, you're not the least bit concerned, are you?"

Delmar could stand it no more and said, "That's quite enough, Shezuka."

Tamahaki got up and stormed off toward her hammock as she said, "I'm getting sick of all this. I'm going to bed."

"What's this I hear coming from you, Delmar?" Shezuka said with a voice of disgust. "What is it about her that regardless of all that you know about her, you still defend her?"

As Prissy was leaving in tears, Delmar said, "Because, Shezuka, I'm in love with her."

"Even though you know she isn't in love with you?" Shezuka questioned more defiantly, hoping to draw Delmar over to her side.

"Yes. Even if she doesn't love me, or ever will love me," Delmar said, hoping that Prissy heard him.

This was more than Shezuka bargained for, and knowing she failed in her mission, she plopped down on the ground and finished her meal.

Delmar reached over and took the bottle they had been using and walked off in the direction of the beach.

Delmar could see Prissy's form a short way down the beach and as he approached, he said, "I wish we could have played a little longer."

Although Prissy was embarrassed and ashamed to be near Delmar, she was polite and asked, "Why's that?"

Delmar said, "Because I wanted to ask Shezuka a personal question about herself."

Prissy stood there for a moment contemplating what in the world Delmar could possibly want to learn about her, so she inquired further as she wiped tears that were running down her cheek, "Oh, and what could there be about her that would interest you?"

"I wanted to know if her horns just fell out after she reached a certain age or if she had them surgically removed," Delmar said as he sat himself down on the beach.

Prissy chuckled and then sat down facing Delmar. "Thanks," she said.

"For what?" Delmar inquired.

"For never changing, Delmar," Prissy said. "For always being my friend, even when I'm not much of one."

Delmar placed the bottle between them and said, "We didn't finish our game."

"What more could you possibly stand to learn about me, Delmar?" Prissy asked with a despairing tone in her voice.

Delmar spun the bottle and it landed on himself, so he said, "The bottle doesn't want me to ask you a question; it wants you to ask me a question."

Prissy looked directly into Delmar's eyes and asked, "What was the worst thing I've done in hurting you?"

Delmar not wanting to answer her, jokingly said, "You can't hurt the man of steel."

"Yes, I can and I have hurt you, Delmar," Prissy confessed.

"It really doesn't matter any longer, Prissy," Delmar said, hoping that his second dodge would end her pursuit to know.

"Please, Delmar," Prissy said as she gently held his hand. "Won't you trust me enough to answer my spin-the-bottle question?"

Delmar exhaled and drooped his shoulders, knowing that he was unable to avoid answering her. He asked, "Remember when we first came in contact with each other over the phone? I was working in the human resources department when you called inquiring if there were any jobs available. I told you that there were no positions available at the moment, but to keep calling and checking in. As you did, we became the best of friends, or so it seemed. You even sent me your picture in an e-mail, but I somehow managed to delete it."

"Yes, I remember all of that, Delmar," Prissy said, "but how does that tie in to me hurting you?"

Delmar continued by saying, "It was just after I sent you my picture that things seemed to change between us and when I sent you a request for you to resend your picture is when you hurt me the most. I never felt so dirty in all my life when you refused to resend it to me. I knew deep down that it was because you didn't like how I looked in the picture I sent to you."

"Oh, Delmar," Prissy said as she got on her knees and began hugging him, "I'm so sorry I did that to you. I honestly had no idea you would have taken it that way."

Delmar gently pulled her toward him, causing her to sit in his lap. With tears running down his face he said, "I'm really glad we played spin the bottle tonight."

"Because?" Prissy asked.

"Because," Delmar continued, "for the first time since we've known each other, something finally gave us a reason to be honest about how we really felt."

Prissy closed her eyes as she continued to hold onto Delmar. As the moments passed pleasurably by, Prissy reached over and took the bottle and placed it upon her lap.

"This," she said, "is the most important object I own."

Delmar looked down at what she had taken off the beach and with wide eyes he said in a panic, "Prissy, I hate to burst your romantic bubble at a time like this, but you just picked up a crab!"

Prissy shrieked as she instinctively flung the crab out of her lap and into the water. In an attempt to save the moment, Prissy quickly regained her composure by acting as though the crab never existed. As she reached for the real bottle, Delmar began to laugh at her. He jokingly said to her, "May I suggest that you spin the bottle first in order to see whether it has legs or not!?"

Prissy giggled as she gave the bottle a spin, then placing it in her lap, she snuggled back into Delmar's chest, reflecting on the quality time she was spending with the man she had come to love and admire.

Chapter Five: Frustrated and Going In

In the third month, Mr. Tyson became frustrated with the way the search had produced nothing.

"That's the last straw," Mr. Tyson said out loud as he slammed the phone on its receiver. "If you want to have the job done right, then you just got to do it yourself," he continued as he buzzed for Rachel on his intercom.

Rachel buzzed back. "Yes, Mr. Tyson?"

"I need you in here right away, Mrs. Holmes," Mr. Tyson said as though he was calling for medical assistance.

Rachel sprang to her feet and dashed into Mr. Tyson's office being almost afraid to enter. "Oh, Mr. Tyson, is everything all right in here?" Rachel questioned like a concerned nurse.

"No, everything is not all right!" he said as he jerked his suit coat off the hanger and whisked it on in one quick motion. "Have my pilot meet me with the plane fueled and ready for departure by the time I get to the airport," he shouted as he was leaving the office in a rage.

"But what about the shareholders' meeting tonight and the board meetings tomorrow and the —" Rachel said in vain as she trailed behind him as he was making his way to the elevator.

As Mr. Tyson continued pressing the down arrow, he cut her off by saying, "Cancel everything until I return."

"And when will that be, sir?" Rachel asked as she cocked her head slightly in a gesture that she was completely confused.

As the door to the elevator opened, Mr. Tyson turned, pushed the button to the first floor, and spoke before the door separated them. "I'll be back," Mr. Tyson said with a serious look in his eyes, "when I have Miss Shoemaker and Mr. Coppertone back safe and sound in our midst." And with that confession, he nodded his head once in a gesture that meant this is an unchangeable decision.

Carlton slowly swept past Rachel and said, "You know how he gets sometimes when he gets mad about something."

"I know," Rachel said running back to her phone. "That's what scares me about this whole thing. I'm calling in reinforcements."

"You go, girl," Carlton said as he stood by her desk and watched her go into action.

Rachel called every salesperson she knew who was available and told them of Mr. Tyson's plan to search for their lost fellow employees. Five Raven Industry employees beat Mr. Tyson to the plane and made themselves at home inside.

As Mr. Tyson entered the plane, he asked, "What's going on here?"

"Sir," one of the salesmen said, "Rachel called and told us what you were about to do, and we are available to help."

With a big smile, he said, "Remind me to put Mrs. Holmes in for a raise when I get back from Asia."

"Will do, chief," the salesman happily agreed.

Mr. Tyson banged on the cockpit door, and the pilot opened it slightly and said, "Yes, Mr. Tyson?"

"I'm in a hurry to get to the Philippines," he said as he sunk back in his chair.

"Philippines coming right up, sir," the pilot said as he radioed the control tower for clearance.

Back on the island, the survivors assembled together in order to determine what should be done to help expedite their rescue.

Shezuka spoke up first, because she was the most irritated at being marooned. "I think that our desperate situation justifies an equally desperate act in order for us to be discovered."

"What are you suggesting we do, Shezuka?" Tamahaki inquired.

Shezuka responded almost insanely, "I think that we should set this God-forsaken island on fire in order to create a large enough smoke cloud to be seen from far away."

"But what about all the animals that live on this island?" Prissy asked.

"Animals!" Shezuka shouted. "Animals? I could care less about a pack of wild animals that live on an uncharted island in the midst of hundreds of other uncharted islands. I'm dirty, I'm hungry, and I'm exhausted from cooking your stinking meals. Now I think that if anybody has earned the right to burn this stinking place to the ground, then that person is me."

Delmar barged in to restore order as he waved both of his hands lower, then lower. "You are both right to some degree. If we set the jungle on fire, we do risk killing the animal population that is here, but what is even worse than that is if the smoke fails to be detected, then we will destroy our only means of shelter and food. However, Shezuka is right in that our only chance of being discovered is to make a smoke signal large enough that it could be seen from a very long distance away."

Tamahaki added, "And yet, if we just make regular smoke from brush, then anyone who sees it will assume that it's just another brush fire on an uninhabited island."

"You're right," Prissy said, as she thought a moment on the obstacle, then snapping her finger she added, "I've got it; what we need is to create some kind of colored smoke."

Everybody began unanimously nodding their heads in agreement to the colored smoke scheme.

"Great. Good work, Sherlock," Shezuki said as though everyone else was making April Fools jokes. "Well, it really was great of you guys to get us through that monstrous dilemma, without having to thumb through too many encyclopedias to solve it."

"Why don't you try for once to be pleasant to her?" Tamahaki asked in a disgusted tone.

"Oh, yeah, little Miss Stick-Up-For-Everybody-Else," Shezuka said in a hateful manner back.

Tamahaki said, "Well, it's obvious that no matter how stranded you are, your character never seems to be affected by it."

"And what is that supposed to mean?" Shezuka asked as she stood up.

"That means," Tamahaki said as she got up herself, "that you are the most emotionally stable person I've ever known."

"Oh, yeah, how so?" Shezuka placed her hands on her hips.

"You're the most emotionally stable person I know because you are always mad and cruel," Tamahaki said placing her hands on her hips.

As Shezuka and Tamahaki continued to verbally tear into each other, Delmar looked over at Prissy with a smile.

Prissy rolled her eyes as if to say, "Here we go again." Delmar cocked his head over toward the direction of the jungle to invite her to join him for a walk in the wild.

Prissy slowly got up, hoping not to disturb her fellow sisters who were completely absorbed in their shouting match. Delmar reached over and pulled Prissy close to him as Prissy reached over and held Delmar's arm.

Delmar asked with a slight tone of laughter in his voice, "You know what?"

"Tell me, dear," Prissy replied with a huge smile on her face.

"I was just thinking how wonderful it is being stuck out here with you," Delmar smirked back.

Prissy replied, "Aw, now that was a sweet thing to say."

"But," Delmar said as though he were the doctor who was now giving the bad news, "being stuck here with those two really causes me to want to get rescued."

Prissy laughed as she said, "Then, let's hope it's really soon."

Chapter Six: Where There's Smoke, There's

Survivors

Mr. Tyson arrived at the airport where his lost employees were during the day of their disappearance.

"Okay, fellows," Mr. Tyson said to get their attention, "while the plane is taking on fuel, we will go have lunch and discuss our next move."

The group sat around a large table and as drinks were being served, Mr. Tyson asked the pilot, "What is the most likely thing that can go wrong that will make a plane fly off its course?"

"Well, I'd have to say possibly a very serious electrical storm with high winds would be about the worst thing I could imagine," said the pilot as he stirred his tea.

"And why is that?" Mr. Tyson inquired as he leaned forward as though this was top secret information.

"I'd have to say that if the storm were powerful enough, it could cause the instrumentation in the plane to fail completely or to lose its precision," clarified the pilot.

"And how bad could that misdirect the plane?" Mr. Tyson pressed.

"Taking in the wind speed and the direction that it was pushing up against the plane, along with calculating in the amount of fuel they must have had and also how scrambled the instruments they were using may have become, I'd say they could have been easily displaced off their true course somewhere in the neighborhood of two hundred miles or more," the pilot said in a logically cold manner.

Mr. Tyson sat back in his seat and turned to his computer wiz, Miles Corbett, and said, "Miles."

Miles, knowing his boss all too well, said in an excited reply, "I'm on it, sir."

"Jeffries," Mr. Tyson said as he turned to face him.

"Uh, yes sir, Mr. Tyson," Jeffries responded back somewhat uneasily.

Mr. Tyson continued, "I hear that you're about the best there is when it comes to math. Is that right?"

Jeffries straightened his tie some as he attempted to sit straighter in his chair. "Well, sir, when I have a calculator in my hand, I don't believe there is a soul on this planet that can match me."

"Good," Mr. Tyson said, just before sipping his tea. "I want you to take your calculator and precisely plot out for me the course that our missing airplane would have taken. Then I want you to figure in the calculations that Miles will come up with once he has researched the weather conditions on the day the plane disappeared."

In between eating their meals, Miles and Jeffries worked together to come up with the most logical guess as to the location of the missing plane.

"Well, what did you two come up with?" Mr. Tyson asked as he finished wiping his mouth with his napkin.

"It looks as though the pilot was a little wrong, sir," Miles replied.

"How wrong?" Mr. Tyson asked pointedly raising an eyebrow at his pilot.

Jeffries jumped in and said, "It appears that the plane went off course closer to 360 miles, or thereabouts, if the wind were at a constant most of the trip."

"Outstanding. Now grab a couple of sandwiches and head to the jet," Mr. Tyson said as he tossed his napkin down. As he placed two one-hundred-dollar bills on the table, he said, "I feel lucky today, boys."

On the island, Delmar and Prissy discussed the many plants that were available and what their possible colors of smoke might be if they were burned.

Discouraged, Prissy cried out, "It's no use, Delmar," then she crouched herself down into a ball. As she began sobbing, she whined, "We're stuck here forever, and there's no way off this miserable rock."

"Rock — that's it, Prissy; that's our solution," Delmar said excitedly. "This island has large deposits of red sandstone."

"So?" Prissy asked confused.

Delmar continued, "We take these soft red rocks down to our camp and pulverized them into tiny particles. Then we soak them with what fuel is still left in the wings of the airplane and scatter them on the top of a large heap of brush. The heat alone should be enough to scatter the tiny flakes far into the atmosphere."

Prissy raised her head and looked straight at Delmar as though she had just come out of a comma, asking, "Well then, what are we waiting for?"

Delmar playfully tackled her and, for a short moment, they forgot their plight as they rolled together on the sand, before racing back to the camp to inform the others of their plan. They became excited and Shezuka started to dig a big burn pit in the sand, while Tamahaki searched for anything flammable. Delmar gathered red sandstone and Prissy pounded them into powder using a hammer that was in the tool chest.

When everything was in place, Delmar cautioned everybody, saying, "Remember, once the fire starts, we have to keep it hot by adding more fuel. I'll toss the fuel soaked die in and you ladies toss wood as it is needed."

"Let's do it," Shezuki said holding a piece of brush in her hand.

Delmar tossed in a burning stick and the pit almost exploded from all the fuel soaking inside of it. The survivors began tossing the fuel soaked sandstone flakes in and the flames jumped sending a big pillar of red-colored smoke into the air.

The brush heap was quickly burning down so Delmar ordered more wood. They frantically kept at this pace for several hours until they had used up all their resources. Exhausted, they reclined on the sand and rested.

Tamahaki cried out, "How long, Delmar, before we know if this trick worked?"

Delmar thought for a moment and then replied, "Honestly, Tamahaki, I'm not totally sure that it will work. I just thought that perhaps we could try to do something besides accept our imprisonment."

"Why shouldn't it work?" Tamahaki inquired further.

"Because," Delmar responded politely, "our smoke will only be seen if a plane is flying overhead."

"Oh, that's just great, Delmar," Shezuka blasted out in disgust. "You inform us of these crucial facts only after we've blow all of our fuel and dead wood on this."

"Calm down, Shezuka; it's not the end of the world," Prissy bit back.

Shezuka jumped to her feet and leapt on Delmar, beating on him as she screamed, "I told you we should have burnt this god-forsaken island to the ground, but no, Mr. Controlled Burning wouldn't have it!"

As the other two ladies worked to remove Shezuka from Delmar, a low-flying plane flew over them. They released Shezuka and started waving their arms in the air, shouting hysterically, "Over here! Over here!"

Shezuka stepped back from Delmar and shrugged her shoulders stating, "Sorry, it's PMS."

Delmar looked up at Shezuka, totally amazed at her drastic mood changes from wild to calm.

Shezuka reached down and offered Delmar a hand up, and Delmar burst out laughing as he accepted her offer, saying, "Shezuka, I know you can go from crazy to calm, but what we really need from you is to go from PMS to S.O.S."

Shezuka patted Delmar on the jaw and laughed out, "Coming right up, big boy," then joyfully Shezuka began jumping up and down, screaming at the top of her lungs like everyone else, "Over here! Over here!"

As the plane flew by again, something was cast out of its cargo door and landed nearby. Running over to the object, they discovered that it was a briefcase. When they opened the briefcase, inside was a note that read, "*We saw the smoke and are sending you help.*"

Attached to the note was a blank check with Mr. Tyson's name on it.

"Unbelievable," Delmar shouted and hopped.

The survivors celebrated the rest of the day until their rescuers arrived.

Chapter Seven: Coconut Vows

One year later, Raven Industries was having their annual progress meeting. As expected, every sales representative in the company was there. Mr. Tyson entered the room and everyone stood and said their hellos as Mr. Tyson warmly shook hands as he made his way to the head of the table.

Mr. Tyson started off the meeting in his usual manner, with his delightful southern charm and compliments. Immediately into his speech, he made a special announcement that surprised everybody, "Ladies and gentlemen, I am pleased to inform you that one year ago, I acquired a luxury property and immediately set out to develop it. I have been told that it is now completed and thus, I would like to extend to everyone present an invitation to come to my grand opening ceremony. All expenses will be paid by Raven Industries for you and your families to attend."

The room erupted with applause and cheers.

Mr. Tyson concluded the meeting with, "In closing, I would like to offer you an opportunity to make any announcements before we conclude this year's business."

There was a moment of silence before Delmar said, "Mr. Tyson, I have an announcement and I think everyone present should know about it."

"Go ahead, son," Mr. Tyson said, unsure of Delmar's notice.

Delmar cleared his throat then, turning towards Prissy, got down on his knees, opened a ring case, and asked, "Prissy Shoemaker, will you marry me?"

Prissy, without even a hint of hesitation, tearfully said, "Yes," as she leaned over and kissed Delmar. As they held each other, the room cheerfully applauded as they offered their support and praise.

Mr. Tyson seized upon the opportunity and asked, "Well, then, if you are getting married, then why not do it at my new resort?"

The couple looked at each other then said, "We'd love to."

To build upon his surprise, Mr. Tyson refused to tell anyone exactly where the new resort was. He rented a commercial jet large enough to transport his entourage over to his private airstrip located next to his resort. Hawaiian music and dancers greeted everyone as they climbed out.

As Delmar pecked Prissy on the forehead, Prissy squeezed him back and said, "This is the most perfect place for a wedding and honeymoon."

Everyone checked in and rested before the big shows that would be offered just as the sun was setting.

That evening, a knock came at Prissy's door.

"Why Mr. Tyson, what a pleasant surprise," Prissy said happily.

"That's what I'm good at," Mr. Tyson responded, "surprises. I just wanted to let you know that there is a nature trail on the west end of the hotel that you should take with Delmar before the sun sets and it becomes too dark to see anything."

"Oh, thanks for the tip, Mr. Tyson. We'll go just as soon as I find Delmar," Prissy assured Mr. Tyson.

Mr. Tyson, with a pleased look on his face, turned and said, "That's just wonderful."

On the nature trail, Delmar stopped and looked intently at the surroundings.

"What is it, Delmar?" Prissy inquired.

Delmar raised his hand as though he could feel the scenery he was taking in and asked, "You ever get the feeling that you've been at a place before, though you know you haven't ever been there?"

Prissy took Delmar's hand and said, "Sometimes."

As they walked further, they came to an area that froze them in their footsteps. Before them was the airplane that they had crashed in and a little beyond it was the beach they often sat at and enjoyed the night breeze.

"Oh my God, Delmar," Prissy said as she ran up to the plane and touched it. "We're back on the island."

Delmar laughed out in amazement at the cunning of Mr. Tyson. As they were laughing at their astonishment, Mr. Tyson came walking down the boardwalk with a minister next to him and a large company of people.

As the crowd encircled them, the minister began to speak about love and commitment. Then, as he began the vows, Prissy and many of the guests started to cry when he asked, "Before God and these witnesses, Delmar Coppertone, do you swear to take Prissy Shoemaker to be your lawfully wedded wife? To love her, to honor her, to cherish her, to support and protect her all the days of your life?"

"I do," said Delmar as he looked into Prissy's eyes.

As they exchanged their vows, the musicians and flame dancers arrived and began to play and dance, and the reception followed at the resort.

Mr. Tyson approached the newlyweds and said to them, "You know, this resort is lacking only one thing for it to succeed."

"And what would that be?" Delmar inquired.

Mr. Tyson pointed his cane toward the resort and said, "Management."

Prissy looked over at her husband and smiled, then together they said, "We'll take the job."

Mr. Tyson chuckled as he drew them both in for a long, compassionate hug. They clung to him as though he was their own father, and in a real way, he was.

Weldon's Stupid Kid

Chapter One: Odessa, 101

I was living in the west of my state in the city of Odessa, Texas. I'm told it began as a tent city mostly made up of Russian immigrants. Odessa and Midland grew so close to each other that some said a day would come when they would become one big city named *Mid-dessa*. I think it would be okay to call it *Mid-dessa* if you're heading west on I-20, but if you're heading east, then you should call the place, *Odd-land*. The news stations we watched dubbed this union the Petroplex, because the region offered its inhabitants sandstorms, tumbleweeds and lots of oil field work. Just a few miles down the road is a sizable desert with nothing but sand dunes for miles in every direction. The old folks called this place *"the end of the world,"* but to an imaginative twelve-year-old, the place wasn't half bad with a little fixing up. I know I did my part when I built a rock dam across the Pecos River underneath a bridge close to the town of Pecos.

My dad was a roughneck in the oil business, as were many of my friends' dads. It was common practice for parents to take their teenage sons out on drilling locations in order to break them in on all the sights and sounds of the drilling process. This was done in order to give them an upper hand when it came their time to get a job. Both my older brothers had been out with my dad several times and so it was assumed that I was ripe for training. Someone should have asked me if I were ready before jumping to such a grand assumption, because as you will soon learn, I wasn't even close.

Chapter Two: Just Getting There

I was on top of the world when my dad told me I was going out the next day with him to a drilling location. My dad liked taking us places because my mom always sent him with a lunch that was made for a king. No little sack, mind you; it was a big grocery sack jammed full of goodies. My mom was very protective of us and she didn't take any chances on us getting stranded out in the desert without enough food to last us until we were rescued. I don't blame her, either, for if I had to go through all the trouble she did to have and raise me, then I'd put some safeguards in place to ensure I made it out alive.

We were standing outside next to the road, waiting for the chauffeur to pick us up. I later found out that his name was Mr. Tool Pusher. Mr. Pusher seemed like a nice guy and all, but he had this really fat cigar in his mouth that smelled up to high heaven. I'm still unsure how he got such a huge cigar between his lips and what's even more puzzling is how anyone understood what he said when he talked. The car we rode in was so well air-conditioned that beef could have been safely stored inside with us. Luck was on my side, because I got to sit in the back with two chunky guys who kept me sheltered from the frozen wind, thus making the trip tolerable. We rode for some forty miles before taking a dirt road that led to the drilling locations. We were pulling the day shift, which made things even better for what I had in mind to do.

We exchanged crews, but there was no rush for the men to scramble to the drilling floor because the drill bit was slowly cutting its way through a difficult layer of rock several hundred feet down and the night shift had taken care of all the chores. Because of all this, the men decided to avoid the blistering heat and so they hung out inside their large tool shed they called the "*doghouse.*" I, for one, wasn't interested in anything adult but was totally committed to finding free stuff, so I could take it home and show everybody my artifacts. My dad really hated for us to bring anything home, because he was afraid we may have taken it from someone's yard. He had a firm policy that if we brought anything home, then he would send us away to put it back where we found it. This was different though, because this stuff was skull bones of dead cows and arrowheads from Apache tribes that roamed the area long ago.

Chapter Three: Oh, Man

As I was racing down the steps away from the doghouse, I heard my dad shout out to me, "Stay away from the creek!" I ran as fast as my imagined bionic legs could go and just as straight as they could go to the creek. *Creek*, I thought to myself, *this would be a great way to cool off and go swimming.* We didn't get to go swimming much in Odessa, unless someone took us to the pool at the County Road West Park. When I got there, I realized that my dad's version of a creek was vastly different from that of my own. This wasn't a swimming creek at all, but a mud creek used to catch all the sludge that came up out of the drilling hole when it pressured out. However, the mud was new to me and I wanted badly to take a sample back for further evaluation. As I stooped over the edge, I reached down to scoop some out when all of a sudden, the embankment collapsed causing me to slide on my back into the miserable goop. "Oh man!" I cussed as I lay there on my back. I thought to myself, *What was a nice kid like me doing in a bad place like this?* I tried the spider method of escape by picking my mid-section up and walking on all fours with no success. Finally, reality set in and I rolled onto my stomach and crawled out of my personalized pit.

I started the long trip back to the drilling rig anguishing over the thought of how my dad was going to clobber me. I slowly made my way up the steps that led to the entrance of the doghouse and when I came into the view of the men inside, I heard them drown out the machinery as they all burst into a roar of laughter. I suppose my dad didn't feel comfortable beating me in front of the other men because I had made them all so wonderfully happy; instead, he just said, "Come on, boy." He escorted me through the doghouse and onto the drilling floor, where to one side was a water hose neatly rolled up and waiting for me. While my dad was spraying me down, one of the men rudely interrupted our quality time and said, "Gee, Weldon, you sure have a stupid kid." My dad chuckled and said back, "Yeah, he's pretty stupid, isn't he?" When the shower ended, my dad ordered me to take all my clothes off except for my underwear so he could hang them on a muffler to dry. While this happened, my seventy-five-pound body sat in a steel doghouse in my dripping underwear, listening to a bunch of hole-punchers torment me about my IQ level.

Chapter Four: Déjà Vu

The clothes dried out really fast and I wasted no time in getting my gear on. I was heading down and away from these oddball people, who obviously knew nothing about what it was like to be a twelve-year-old boy. As I ran down the steps, I heard my dad shout at me once again, "Stay away from the creek!" Yeah, yeah, what did he think I was — stupid or something? I actually had every intention of staying away from the creek, but I really needed to know what went wrong at the accident site, so I could return with my findings and forever clear my name as Weldon's stupid kid.

There I was, at the exact location of my mishap, utilizing my TV detective skills. As I was singing the *Hawaii Five-0* theme song, I determined that the ground was loose where I had stood and that it wasn't able to support my weight. As I continued my experiments, I stood over the same place where I first fell in and pushed with my feet with nothing happening. *This sure feels like it's firm enough*, I thought to myself. Frustrated at this, I began jumping up and down on this spot, but there was no cave-in, which proved that I had done everything humanly possible to keep mud off me, but fate would not let me be mud free. Before I darted off to tell the crew about my findings, I squatted down and reached over to get myself another nice big scoop of mud that I tried to get earlier. Just as success was in my sight, the ground crumbled below me. I tried to kick my way back, but the earth just swallowed me up and there — for a second time — I lay on my back in a bed of mud. "Ah, rats," I cussed. I was really mad at myself this time and I wasn't looking forward to getting out, because the water hose was through the doghouse and on the drilling platform. As I lay there trying to figure out the best way to fix this new problem, a snake slithered by me, giving me more than ample motivation to roll over and scramble out of the creek.

On my long walk back to the drilling rig, I was evaluating how much I hated mud. I was also thinking how much I didn't want to be me anymore as I slowly made my way up the steps to the doghouse door. When I reached the top of the steps, an explosion of laughter and howls came rushing out at me. I knew these people didn't have anything else to do out here except to pry into my own personal business, so it was really working out to be a long day. My dad was gleaming with pride before the rest of the men. As he walked toward the water hose, I heard him say once again, "Come on, boy." I knew the routine well enough by then and began the rotisserie chicken while my dad performed an authentic Indian rain ceremony called, *Water Weldon's Stupid Kid So He'll Grow Up Quicker*.

The men who worked with my dad were beyond the realm of annoying as they spent the whole wash time making smooching noises and catcalls at me. My dad just laughed along as every last roughneck went out of his way to remind my dad just how stupid he thought I was. "Man-O-Live," I huffed, "these old dudes are really getting on my nerves." I took off all unnecessary clothing and draped it over the muffler pipe. In my soggy underwear, I sat down inside the doghouse with my head between my legs and my hands covering my ears, but my skinny hands failed to provide enough meat to block out their voices, so once again I found myself as the sole ray of happiness these men could reflect on, out in the middle of nowhere.

By this time, my dad realized I was unable to keep mud off myself, so he grounded me to the doghouse for the rest of the day. How bad could life get for a boy with a need for speed? Here I was, at a noisy drilling rig, grounded to the confines of a large metal tool shed, being inhumanely caged in the middle of a desert, with fat guys poking stupid jokes at me every chance they got. I swore a holy oath on that day that I would never become a roughneck when I got older.

Chapter Five: Say It Isn't So

When my clothes dried out for the second time, I attempted a desperate move to get away from all these jolly jokers, so I told my dad I had to use the number one. He granted me leave and as I was flying down the steps to reach Mother Earth, I heard my dad yell out to me, "Stay away from the mud pit!"

"Mud pit," I yelped to myself in utter horror! There's not a fat chance in Pecos I'd go near anything that begins with the word, *mud.* To my great delight, there in front of me was a dirt clod mound made for a king's son. The mound must be from the pit my dad was warning me to avoid and sure enough — just as I suspected — there on the other side of the hill was a real-to-life, square mud pit. I'm not sure what the mud was for, but I had no intention of ever getting close to it to find out. Staining my clothes and reputation twice was the only cross that anyone my age should ever be expected to bear.

Needless-to-say, there were some really nice dirt clods scattered all over the mound and I found them all too irresistible to walk away from. I climbed to the top of clod hill and imagined that my dirt clods were rockets that I was shooting at enemy troops. As they slammed into metal objects, they would explode into trillions of pieces and the excitement of my missile barrage only intensified. Nothing was spared from me pelting it with a clod rocket. I got so caught up in my rocket war that I lost all track of time and what I had actually come outside for. Without any warning, my dad surprised me as he began yelling at me. I flew off the top of the hill away from him and, you guessed it, into the mud pit he earlier told me to stay away from. As I entered the mud, one of my arms grabbed the side of the pit and when my head came out of the mud, I screamed, "Daddy, save me!" My dad rushed over and reached down and jerked me out like I weighed nothing to him. He continued to hold me as he kicked me across the rear end. I somehow broke loose and began running for dear life and it was my dad I feared who was going to end it. He was yelling while attempting to kick me at the same time, but because I was covered in mud and in motion, he was never able to establish a good hold on me.

I beat my dad to the steps that lead up to the doghouse and when I reached the top, I dashed through it in full view of the men who were still inside. Before my dad could reach me, I grabbed the water hose and turned it on, spraying myself vigorously. As I turned, I shouted out to the men watching, "Y'all come out and take a look at Weldon's stupid kid." My dad and the rest of the men were laughing so hard that they had to lean on each other just to keep from collapsing on the floor. I never heard a pack of coyotes howl as much as they did that day. For the third time, I failed to get the belt lashing that was customary for such offenses. Perhaps it was too messy to beat me covered in mud and it was clearly inappropriate to beat me in soggy underwear. Regardless of the reason why, I was glad that by the time my clothes had dried out, he had calmed down enough not to care about the punishment phase. By then, the men had things to do, and one-by-one, they disbanded, giggling like a bunch of girls at a Valentine's dance. I'd pop my head out just to see the world I was missing and everywhere one of the men was working, I'd see him stop, burst out laughing, then work some more and it was then that I realized that I was in the midst of insanity.

Chapter Six: Angels We Have Heard on High

Although I never got the beatings I knew I deserved, I was never again allowed to go on a job site with my dad. He knew better than to think I was capable of being anything other than a kid who got into more trouble than he could get out of. Many times after our one-time outing, my dad would walk by me and ask with a big smile on his face, "How's it going, Muddy?" It was his special way of not letting me forget that horrible day at the drilling rig.

As time moved on, both my parents became sick and died. Dad died when I was seventeen and Mom passed when I was twenty-one. I was driving home one rainy day when I had a blowout. "Ah, rats," I cussed, "the back right tire is flat!" Instead of waiting for it to quit raining, I got out and jacked up the truck, unbolted the tire, but the tire wouldn't slide off the lug bolts. There just happened to be a deep trench behind me with no grass to cover it and when I jerked the tire to get it off the hub, I lost my footing and there I went sliding down the mud creek once more. As I lay there on my back, I stared into the heavens and pondered just how loud they must be laughing it up over there. I'm almost sure that when I finally get to those pearly gates, I'll see my dad standing at the door waiting for me with a water hose in his hands.

Poetry

Lisa Moo Moo Marie

If I were a bull out in the field
I'd tell you with outright glee
Of a gal who is a pretty good heifer
Lisa Moo-Moo Marie.

I like it when she starts to talk
For it's such a beautiful sound,
Her words are sweeter than alfalfa grass
That shoots up from the ground.

If I were placed inside a stall
I'd still be just as free
For I'm never afraid to be caged
With Lisa Moo-Moo Marie.

She's busier than a herd of steer
On a long cattle drive,
Yet, she always has plenty of time
For my irritating rawhide.

As we grow older, faces being thinner
Our eyes barely able to see
I'd have such a thrill just being still
With Lisa Moo-Moo Marie.

Strolling with her on a dirt trail
Side-by-side and neck-to-neck
I'd gladly breathe a ton of dust
Just to join her in the trek.

And when we get boxed at the packing plant
In heaven I'd like to be
With the best little cowgirl I ever met
Lisa Moo-Moo Marie.

Battle the Beast

The night came quicker than usual
And it caught me by surprise
Before I found some shelter
The blackness dimmed my eyes.

My panicked heart was racing
My legs instinctively took flight
I aimlessly ran in circles
In the horror of blackest night.

In the distance, I could see it
The form of a terrible beast
I could hear its claws scratching
I could see the flash of its teeth.

There was no way to outrun it
For it traveled on all fours
So left with just one prospect
I turned and faced the noise.

The blade I held had a faint sparkle
Illumined from distant stars
The beast knew I would use it
As it stalked me from afar.

My wait dragged on for eternity
As I firmly stood my ground
But soon it would be over
For I heard approaching sounds.

Throughout my life, I purposefully planned
To never travel by night
It was the only way to miss the beast
And avoid a deadly fight.

Yet life has a sense of justice
Not willing to let me cheat those plans
From facing the beast who stalks me
From facing what haunts a man.

A silhouette sprang out of the blackness
Striking hard the first blow
I volleyed back with the tip of my blade
Causing the beast to moan.

Collapsing together, mortally wounded
The dawn began to break
I saw the beast that had attacked me
It was myself in whom I faced.

Ode of Devotion

"Here, sir," the lady said, as she gave me a drink to quench my thirst.

She tended to my most desperate need, when things were at their worst.

"Thank you, dear," I said with a bow, no longer prideful that I was a man.

What could I boast but blood and war, compared to such kind, gentle hands?

She spread her blanket upon the grass then sat against a tree.

Patting her lap, she spoke once more, "Come, recline on me."

Her lap became my pillow, as I fell deep into a trance.

I dreamed we were in a palace, as for hours we laughed and danced.

Awakened by the noise of riders, of people who did not care for her good,

Seizing her, they galloped away, showering me with dust where I stood.

The Magistrate found her guilty and ordered that she pay the full price.

He opened his window above the dungeon so he could hear her beg throughout the night.

"Nay, my Lord, do not harm her, for she is my dearest friend.

I have sworn to heaven to protect her, all the way to the end."

"'Tis well, sir, for I care not, of whom in anguish I hear plea.

Bind this man and take him down and let the woman go free."

Throughout the night they cut me, so often that I knew each blade by name.

I learned their lengths and contours; I knew their specific pains.

Never did I cry because of my sufferings, instead I shouted out the oaths that I had made.

On hearing these, my lady called back, promising she would forever stay.

No longer willing to hurt me, my tormentors were broken from what they heard.

It was they who had been tortured, as we spoke of our devotion in every word.

The magistrate ordered my release, having suffered himself from our good deeds.

He begged our forgiveness and then issued the following decree:

"Be it known that from this day forth, friendship and devotion must be kept."

Whereupon hearing of this new law, the people joyfully wept.

A room was provided for my lady and on a stretcher they brought me in.

And as soon as my dearest touched me, my wounds began to mend.

Appearing at our doorway, a herald brought word from the magistrate

Saying, "My Lord requires your presence in the ballroom, with great haste."

Entering the ballroom under an archway, made from the soldiers touching lance to lance.

The dream I had was now coming true, as for hours we laughed and danced.

Chef's Surprise

Its tail whipped the darkened storm clouds
Causing thunder to rip through the air
Coasting to a hole at the side of a mountain
The dragon returned to its lair.

Blood encircled its mouth
Because its hunt was a success
"The children no longer have milk!"
Said the mother in great distress.

The officer reported the disturbance
To the lord of the land
The king knew it would be costly
If the matter wasn't brought to an end.

A meeting was quickly summoned
The knights gathered in the great hall
But none felt himself able
To fight both fire and iron claws.

The chef who was serving their table
Said he could do the job with ease
But the nobles were insulted by such a claim
So they tossed him out on the street.

There was no time for self-pity
So the chef gathered herbs and spice
In the kitchen he mixed up a brew
Then sneaked off into the night.

In a valley below the mountain
He filled a large caldron with his stew
The dragon sniffed, stretched out his wings
And down to the caldron he flew.

The flavor was so delightful
That the dragon ate every bite
Then out stepped the chef with his spoon
Challenging the dragon to a fight.

The dragon was mocked and angry
He tried slicing the chef with his tail
But the chef jumped into the caldron
And inside he rolled down the hill.

The dragon froze in his steps and was hardened
And a statue he became evermore
This also was the fate of the knights
And also of their lord.

Thus the chef inherited the kingdom
And from his throne this is what he saw
Statues of a king, some knights and a dragon
Lining both sides of the great hall.

The Fisherman and the Weaver

The fisherman was old and weary
His life being full of care
His boat often leaked when out
And his net would sometimes tear.

The catch of fish was slim, he thought
Only enough to feed him for the day
So, not knowing what else to do
He folded his hands to pray.

By chance the weaver heard him
As he walked along the dock
And during the night he wove him a net
From the best he had in stock.

Then taking some pitch
He patched up the fisherman's boat
Then tied it to a nearby post
Using a brand new rope.

The fisherman awoke in thanksgiving
As he surveyed his new net
And when he saw his patched up boat
He got on his knees and wept.

In time also the weaver,
Himself, fell into great need
And not knowing what else to do
He folded his hands to plead.

Rising up early the next morning
What he saw brought tears to his eyes
Outside his door was a barrel
With fish swimming inside.

The Priest and the Executioner

The priest had a troublesome assistant
That he didn't especially like
It wasn't uncommon for their debates
To break out into a fight.

They disagreed on everything
About what the Bible said
From Adam and Eve, all the way through
To the resurrection of the dead.

The priest could take it no longer
Frustrated, he quit the church
And being unskilled he floundered
Unable to survive on commoner's work.

It was his want for food and clothing
That first drove him to steal
He became accustomed to lying
Some claiming he had also killed.

In time he was branded an outlaw
With a hefty price on his head
The reward paid the same amount
Regardless of alive or dead.

Someone found his hideout
Where he was taken to the dungeon
He was offered no food or water
For tomorrow would be his execution.

Early the next morning
He was led off to the stocks
The prosecution found him guilty
So he was led to the chopping block.

He cried out for mercy
But none was to be found
Then came the executioner
At the cheering of the crowd.

He raised his ax high above
But before he could swing
He stopped to join in a hymn
That the priest had started to sing.

Then, one-by-one, the onlookers
Joined them in their song
Revival swept through the crowd
And the priest was pardoned his wrongs.

The executioner helped the priest to his feet
And his bonds he quickly untied
Then upon removing his hood
They were all in for a shocking surprise.

It was the priest's quarrelsome assistant
Who was the one holding the ax
With faith renewed he returned to the church
The assistant also went back.

And for the rest of their lives
The two were the closest of friends
For mercy was beyond an argument
Which caused their hearts to mend.

The Barrel Maker

The black plague troubled Europe
Killing hundreds every day
They quickly burned their bodies
Too many to be given graves.

Yet, a worthy lord had also died
Who ruled his people with kind deeds
He was allowed to be buried
Underneath his favorite tree.

Upon entering the casket shop
It was learned the owner had also died
And to their disappointment
No more coffins remained inside.

It was improper to lay their lord
Without a casket in the ground
Because of this, they all agreed
Another way had to be found.

There was only one other craftsman
Who had managed to survive the plague
It was the aged old cooper
Who was the maker of barrels and kegs.

He compassionately understood their dilemma
And steadily worked throughout the night
His first and only coffin
Was ready by morning's first light.

It was the grandest of all funerals
That took place on the castle green
They buried their lord in a barrel
The longest that had ever been seen.

The Thief and the Sheriff

It's not that thieves are dangerous
To either life or the crown
But they are still scoundrels
That must be hunted down.

The sheriff made a posse from the vendors
Thinking they would be a greater help
It was their businesses that suffered
Their losses being sorely felt.

Just yesterday someone noticed
Vegetables missing from a stand
Then what was left of a wedge of cheese
Looked like a small pile of sand.

We found partially eaten apples
That were tossed out onto the street
There's also been a loss of other things
Like breads, fruits, and meats.

That's why for all these sorrows
In which the thief has done
When finally caught, he'll pay the price
And publicly be hung.

The people will be glad to celebrate
As the gallows get prepared
None will venture to stay home
For surely they'll all be there.

The sheriff will follow protocol
And allow him to speak one last time
Then as if he had no heart at all
He'll hang him for his life of crime.

The deputies arrested someone suspicious
That they thought they could blame
But a child uncovered the truth
While playing her favorite game.

Her ball knocked over a leaning board
Which behind was a nest of rats
The sheriff fired all his deputies
Then employed a dozen cats.

The Blacksmith and the Soldier

His hammer stayed busy that week
Fashioning raw steel into a sword
He took it personally this time
Because he knew who it was for.

It was one thing altogether
To beat things into a useful shape
Yet quite another matter, indeed,
In knowing who will rely on its blade.

Never had there been a blacksmith
Who put such care into making one thing
The sword he made for the commoner
Was worthy to be owned by a king.

Not willing to trust his own skill
He had it blessed by the Pope
And when the soldier learned of this
He departed for the war with more hope.

For months the blacksmith wondered
What was the outcome of the war
Would the soldier find his way back
Or die on a foreign shore?

The soldier returned and spoke openly
Concerning all that he had done
The blacksmith cried as he hugged him
The sword had protected his son.

The Tavern Master and the

Stranger

Merry-makers all became quiet
As the stranger stepped through the door
They looked at each other and pondered
How could he burn footsteps on the floor?

He dropped a red hot coin on the counter
And asked for something cold
Said he had just passed through hell again
Looking for misplaced souls.

Chilled water from the well was brought
And a tall glass put before him
Then as he began to swallow
Steam rose up off his skin.

The patrons were astonished
And one ventured to ask his profession
He said he was a seeker of misplaced souls
Accidentally cast into damnation.

Some scoffed and called him a trickster
But others did believe
The hard-of-heart charged him
To prove his words or leave.

He began naming names of persons
Who from among them had died;
He spoke about their anguish
And the words he heard them cry.

Ending the story with one last drink
He left the way he came
And not too long afterword
The patrons did the same.

The tavern master made a sign
And hung it on a nail
It read, "No longer in business,
For I believe there is a hell."

The town began to prosper
Into a place that others desired
They built the largest churches
They had the biggest choirs.

And as it was their custom
They kept water chilled icy cold
Just in case a stranger happened to mention
He was a seeker of misplaced souls.

Battle Formations

A messenger called the men to hurry
Safely within the nearby castle
The valley would be red once more
From another bloody battle.

The older warriors were the remnant
Of past confrontations
The inexperienced followed their lead
Forming up battle formations.

The sixth commandment they openly forsook
Plotting how best to inflict their pain
Side-by-side marching together
Ready to kill or be slain.

Horns blasted, while voices shouted
Proclaiming the other's doom
Policies would be settled this day
By who inflicts the greater wound.

The clamor of war diminishes
As another body hits the ground
Like cords of wood they lay there
Scattered all around.

Their lives were altogether precious
But were so cheaply taken away
By the demands of others who ruled them
Reducing them back to clay.

The priest cited the obvious text,
"Ashes to ashes and dust to dust,"
As the vultures reminded the living
The cost of misguided trust.

Rulers dined voluptuously
As though nothing had been lost
While families mourn in anguish
From the war's high cost.

Their lords offer a toast to the dead
With no sense of personal condemnation
For causing innocent men to die
In their wretched battle formations.

The Serf and the Ranger

My two sons clash their sticks
As though they were noblemen's swords
They dream of riches and glory
And some day being called a lord.

I haven't the heart to tell them
They weren't born equal and free
Not having the right to ever become
That which they choose to be.

Never have I scolded them
But allowed them to continue their play
For toil and fear will soon arrive
When they dread their manly days.

The children surround a hooded stranger
Who appeared out of the mist
He is a ranger from the forest
Who is on the king's wanted list.

Rangers are considered outlaws
For they answer to no man
They do not slave for others
But live freely off the land.

He lifts his hood and looks at me
Squarely in the eyes
He senses my concern and anguish
Due to my sons' bitter lives.

He tosses a bag of coins in my hand
That he took from the tax collector
Proving to all who were present
He will be our secret protector.

What a noble calling it is
To give strength unto the poor
To dry up tears of those who suffer
Who could not go on any more.

I offered both my sons to him
But he wisely took but one
Leaving me the younger
To care for his parents' home.

As they headed toward the trees
My eldest raised his make-believe sword
His brother obliged and raised his back
Then returned to his chores.

And every time it seemed to us
That we would never see them again
Out of the trees came two hooded rangers
With bags of coins in their hands.

The Cobbler and the Traveler

He slides the blade through the leather
Like a skimmer across the seas
His mind is filled with measurements
Of the one he strives to please.

How wide, how long, how high, how heavy
Are all factored in
Everything must be just right
If it is to grace the feet of men.

In three days, the patron said
He'd be passing back this way
The boots must be finished and fit just right
Before he is willing to pay.

His bed is left empty
As his nights are like his day
Hands and tools never stopping
Except to occasionally pray.

"Grant me strength to carry on,
For I am weak from lack of rest.
Help me to make my deadline,
And the fit is at its best."

And just as he said, on the third day
The traveler returned to the store
And there he saw his lovely boots
When he stepped through the door.

The traveler sat upon a cushion
As the cobbler humbly kneeled
Sliding the boots onto his feet
His satisfaction he revealed.

"Well done, my faithful servant,
Your craftsmanship pleases your king.
Arise now and follow,
For you shall work only for me."

And so it was that the cobbler
Did what his master bid him do
From that day on the king and his lords
Wore only the cobbler's shoes.

The Champion

Faces stained with joyless tears
Their lives in sorrow, be
Tormentors arrived to vex them
Punishing those who try to leave.

Children forgot their sweet dreams
For hardship takes them away
Parents grieving for loss of hope
Not sure of the coming day.

But as the fog began to clear
Toward the range in the east
Sat a figure upon his steed
Who never knew defeat.

But what could he do against the cruel
Who stole freedom away?
Surely one blade against so many
Would rush him to an early grave.

He raised a horn to his lips
And blasted out a mighty sound
The number of knights who followed
Sent shock waves through the ground.

Together they shouted out their plans
Their standards fluttered in the rush
They came to dash the cruel of heart
Bringing vengeance upon the unjust.

The wicked responded quickly
Shooting arrows of flaming hate
But shields and armor cheated death
As the knights reached the main gate.

With hooks and ropes and horses
They dragged the main gate away
The screams and carnage that followed
Ushered in a new and wonderful age.

The wicked were piled in massive heaps
Their fires illumined the night
While the faces of those who were saved
Shone brightly from freedom's light.

Very early in the morning
Just before the sun filled the sky
Back into the fog they headed
Leaving but one upon his ride.

He spun his horse toward us
Placing his fist upon his chest
It was his final act of kindness
Before he joined the rest.

Shouting, "God's speed to you!"
Then victoriously he rode away
Leaving peace and hope behind him
So we could embrace the coming day.

Grateful

Autumn pale, labyrinth skies
Passage to your soul through your eyes.

Ancient desert, endless sands
Soft, gentle touches from your hands.

Unfathomed mysteries, ocean depths
Words and kisses from your lips.

Cool, clean breezes, winter's air
Thoughtful deeds showing me you care.

Majestic mountains, snowy peaks
Long embraces, cheek to cheek.

Giant tree, sheltering bark
Love and honor within your heart.

Life and death, mixed together
Shared with you so much better.

Spare Me

Spare me your frequent bowing and the prayers you claim are for peace

While behind our backs you despise us, scheming methods of war in your sleep

Spare me your Koran reading and your efforts to obey the five pillars

For God has never been master of those who hate and murder.

Spare me your frequent chanting and the wisdom you claim brings peace

While your exalted state of mind commits more war crimes, as bodies litter the streets

Spare me all your enlightenment and your claims of being one with creation

For Shang-Ti and Buddha have called you to love, yet your deeds prove your damnation.

Spare me your chorus singing and the sermons that speak of peace

While your prisons stay full from the victims you've killed and survivors can only weep

Spare me your holy scriptures, for it has not changed your ways

For Jehovah and Christ called you to love your neighbor, but this you have never obeyed.

Spare me your political speeches and the treaties you claim produce peace

For the very same hands push bayonets in men, in order to stop their heartbeat

Spare me your laws and vast learning and how you think it will make us unite

For peace will never be possible, when people desire to fight.

Bowl of Beans

I prayed over a bowl of beans today
For it meant I lived while others died
With every spoonful I acknowledged
That I had what others were deprived.

I cried over a bowl of beans today
For I knew many did not have this to eat
With every morsel I swallowed hard
The suffering of others made me weep.

I handed someone a bowl of beans today
To the hungry it was a great deal
With helping others in their grief
It caused my own heart to heal.

Against Me

There is a voice that cries out against me
In all I do it beckons me to fail
It chants a liturgy called *Excuses*
As it attempts to cast me under its spell.

There is a weight that is set against me
Trying to drag me down into despair
Burdens that keep me from doing much
Pressuring me to lose heart and not care.

There is a host that is unleashed against me
Mighty forces waging war against my mind
Constant battles keeping me distracted
Strategies that use up life's limited time.

Yet, there is a faith that is working for me
It only hears words that say, "You can."
It has the strength that never stops trying
It has the courage to achieve all that it plans.

Wanting and Not Having

An unrewarding job it is, to want and not have
Endeavoring to always get, can drive a person mad.

The acquisition of money, though it appears a noble goal
Fails the steward of such wealth from satisfying his soul.

For on the bed of certain death, his mind can only reflect
Of how he lived to have more things, while dying with such regrets

Like, often passing his children, as they joyfully played their games
But never did he play with them, for his wanting never changed.

The cost for wanting and not having, always put his future at stake
So the only thing that he could do was work to secure his estate.

When he thinks he has enough, he ends his solitude and toil
And with a misguided gleam in his eye, he reaches for his spoil.

But just as soon as he takes it, and shows all his wonderful prize
The luster begins to fade away and the sparkle dims from his eyes.

Sadly now, at the end, he is finally able to believe
That all he gave his life to have, was never going to please.

Slowly passing from this world, he grieves over how he behaved
Because all his wanting and not having, made him nothing more
than a slave.

Come Back To Me

Come back to me my precious darling
Do not think it's too late to try
For as long as there is life within us
Hope and love do not have to die.

My mind is lost in the expanse between us
Fearing you have found relief in tossing us away
With all that we've shared in life together
How is it you found no reason to stay?

Why haven't you come back to me, my precious darling?
Do not think it's too late to try
For as long as there is life within us
Hope and love do not have to die.

You left, it seems, feeling okay about it
Encouraged that you did all that you could
But you left me on my knees still begging
Leaving me to wonder where it was you stood.

Can't you come back to me, my precious darling?
Do not think it's too late to try
For as long as there is life within us
Hope and love do not have to die.

The winter blast from your cold heart chills me
No amount of sunny words can thaw me out
For unless they come from my darling partner
There can be no warmth, this far south.

Shouldn't you come back to me, my precious darling?
Do not think it's too late to try
For as long as there is life within us
Hope and love do not have to die.

Let us melt away those cold feelings
As we nurse dead stems back to life
Forget the debt we have charged each other
Let our arms tenderly hold each other tight.

Come back to me, my precious darling
Do not think it's too late to try
For as long as there is life within us
Hope and love will never die.

Special Gift

When I was young I used to pray
Before I'd sleep or start a new day
For a special gift that I could hold
That I could love from the depth of my soul.

It would take a miracle to bring her my way
That's why, in faith, I began to pray
Years passed by, everything was the same
Then a girl said, "Hi," and she told me her name.

I wondered in amazement as I listened to her
How similar in feelings we both were
With each passing moment the truth became clear
She was my prayer's answer that I should hold dear.

So I gave her my heart and she gave me hers
And when we pray these words can be heard:

When we were young we used to pray
Before we'd sleep or start a new day
For a special gift that we could hold
Someone we could love from the depths of our soul.

Life

Life is meaningless if death is all
What one inherits when it's recalled.

It makes no difference about your caste
How much you're worth, how long you last.

All we gather in toil and pain
Comes to naught, death robs all gain.

Great success can mark our days
But come tomorrow, it fades away.

Physical life would be a meaningless deceit
If death was only an eternal sleep.

What keeps us going is that there's more
At the time we pass death's blighted door.

Wake up you sluggard and become alive
Bring value to your efforts before you die.

You ask, "What gives life its greatest success?"
Why, it's living for God, while doing our best.

Servant's Creed

To die a little more each day
Helps me to learn how to obey.

In doing those things that you say
I'll die myself a little more each day.

And as a bird learns to fly
That from its nest it must die

The one who never soars up high
Does he fear death, who never tries?

In order to carry a servant's tray
I must put to death my selfish ways.

And only then should I begin to pray
For others to die a little more each day.

Blind Without a Cause

The worst blindness is not from the eyes, but minds that refuse to see

They shut out everything they don't like, no matter how sound it may be

Brick by brick, they stack a wall up to heaven, not allowing the glorious light to shine through

They say to God, "Don't bother us and we won't bother you."

They applaud their own ingenuity and boast that they are wise

They live any way that they see fit, because darkness covers their eyes

Plague after plague may befall them, as they stumble year after year

They tell all who are watching, "There's absolutely nothing to fear."

They till, they plant, they gather their harvest, building bigger and better barns

They recline in comfort and proclaim to themselves, "Relax and enjoy all that's been earned."

With a smile on their lips, they lie on their beds, thinking, *Darkness has worked out okay.*

But the angel of death appeared and said, "You won't live to see a new day!"

They die and awake in anguish and throughout the ages you can hear their cries

For ever and ever, they curse their choices, of letting darkness cover their eyes

Yet the Creator so loves every person, that, to earth, his Son was sent

Not desiring that any should perish, but from darkness mankind would repent.

Praying

As I kneel beside my bed
With my eyes open wide
I see no form around me
Yet I know he's by my side.

I never question my sanity
As it seems I speak into thin air
There are no doubts that haunt me
For I know he's truly there.

I get so much off my chest
As in prayer I reverently speak
About my day's happenings
With its victories and defeats.

I can think of no greater comfort
Than knowing he patiently hears
All my thoughts that I share
In praises and in tears.

So always remind me, dear Lord,
Before I go to sleep
To never allow my eyes to close
Until you in prayer I seek.

CPSIA information can be obtained at www.ICGtesting.com
Printed in the USA
LVOW12*1957100415

434002LV00003B/5/P